March Hares

Harold Frederic

March Hares
First published in London in 1896
Copyright © 1896 Appleton and Company

Cover Art: London Romance

First Edition

AN: 9 8 7 6 5 4 3 2 1

ISBN-10: 1943341044
ISBN-13: 978-1943341047

Contents

Chapter 1

On the morning of his thirtieth birthday, David Mosscrop lounged against the low stone parapet of Westminster Bridge, and surveyed at length the unflagging procession of his fellow-creatures plodding past him northward into the polite half of London town.

He had come upon the bridge in a melancholy frame of mind, and had paused first of all gloomily to look down at the water. His thoughts were a burden to him, and his head ached viciously.

This was no new experience of a morning, worse luck; he had grown accustomed to these evil opening hours of depression and nausea. The fact that it was his birthday, however, gave uncomfortable point to his reflections.

He had actually crossed the threshold of the thirties, and he came into the presence of this new lustrum worse than empty-handed. He had done none of the great things which his youth had promised. He had not even found his way into helpful and cleanly company.

The memory of the people with whom he spent his time nowadays—in particular, the recollection of the wastrels and fools with whom he had started out yesterday to celebrate the eve of his anniversary—made him sick.

He stared down at the slowly-moving flood, and asked himself angrily why a man of thirty who had learned nothing worth learning, achieved nothing worth the doing; who didn't even know enough to keep sober overnight, should not be thrown like garbage into the river.

The impulse to jump over the parapet hung somewhere very close to the grasp of his consciousness. His mind almost touched it as his eyes dwelt upon the broad, opaque mass of shifting drab waters. He said to himself that he had never before been so near the possibility of deliberate suicide as he was at this moment.

He did not allow the notion to take any more definite shape, but mused for a while upon the fact of its lying there, vaguely formless at the back of his brain, ready to leap into being at his will.

Of course, he would not give the word: it was merely interesting to think that he was in the same street, so to speak, with the spirit of self-murder.

After a little, the effect of this steadily drifting body of water seemed to soothe his vision. He grew less conscious of mental disturbance and physical disgust alike. Then he stood up, yawned, and glanced at the big clock-tower, where the laggard hands still clung to the unreasonable neighborhood of seven o'clock.

For some reason, he felt much better. The sensation was very welcome. He drew a long breath of satisfaction, and, leaning with his back to the stonework, fell to watching the people go past.

By a sudden revulsion of mood, he discovered all at once that the excess of the night was now offering him compensations. His brain was extremely clear, and, now that the lees of drink were gone, served him with an eager and almost fluttering acuteness which it was pleasant to follow.

He noted with minute attention the varying types of workmen, shopgirls, clerks, and salesmen as they trooped by in the throng, and found himself devoting to each some appropriate mental comment, some wondering guess into their history, or some flash of speculation as to their future.

The instantaneous play of his fancy among these flitting items brought great diversion. He rollicked in it—picking out as they trudged along side by side the book-keeper who was probably short in his accounts, the waiter who had been hacking the wrong horses, the barmaid with the seraph's face who at luncheon time would be listening unmoved to conversation from City men fit to revolt a dock laborer.

It was indeed as good as a play, this marvelous aggregation of human dramatic possibilities surging tirelessly before him. He wondered that he had never thought of seeing it before.

From amusing details his mind lifted itself to larger conceptions. He thought of the mystery of London's vast economy; of all its millions playing dumbly, uninstructedly, almost like automata, their appointed parts in the strange machinery by which so many droves of butchers' cattle, so many thousands of tons of food and trucks of clothing and coals and oil were brought in daily, and Babylon's produce was sent out again in balancing repayment.

The miracle of these giant scales being always kept even, of London's ever-craving belly and the country's never-failing response, loomed upon his imagination.

Then, stifling another yawn, it occurred to him that a brain capable of such flights deserved a better fate than to be banged out by a dirty tide against some slime-stained wharf-pile down the river. Yes, and it merited a nobler lot in life, too, than that of being nightly drenched with poisonous drink. Decidedly he would forswear sack, and live cleanly.

The hour struck in the clock-tower. The boom of the great bell swelled hopefully upon his hearing. The chime of the preceding quarter had saddened him, because he heard in it the knell of thirty wasted years.

The louder resonance now bore a different meaning. A birthday exposed a new leaf as well as turned down an old one. The twenties were behind him, and undoubtedly they were not nice. Very well; he turned his back upon them. The thirties were all before him; and, as Big Ben thundered forth its deep-voiced clamor, he straightened himself, and turned to look them confidently in the face.

His eyes fell upon the figure of a young woman, advancing in a little eddy of isolation from the throng, a dozen feet away. Even on the instant he was conscious of a feeling that his gaze had not distinguished her from the others by mere chance; it was, indeed, as if there were no others.

In the concentrated scrutiny which he found himself bending upon her, there was a sense of compulsion. His perceptions raced to meet and envelop her.

She was almost tall, and in carriage made the most of her inches. She had much yellow hair of a noticeable sort, pale flaxen in bulk but picked with lemon in its lights, about her brows. He thought that it was dyed, and in the same breath knew better.

He mastered the effect of her fine face—with its regular contour, its self-conscious eyes, its dainty rose-leaf of a chin thrust reliantly forth above a broad, white throat—all in some unnamed fraction of a second.

The impression of her filled every corner of his mind. He tried to think about who and what she was, and only built up scaffoldings of conjecture to knock them down again.

She was a girl who tried on mantles and frocks in some big Regent Street place: no, the lack of dignity in such an avocation would be impossible to one who carried her chin so high.

A woman journalist? No, she was too pretty for that. What was she—type-writer, restaurant-waitress, saleswoman? No, these all wore black, with white collar and wristbands; and her apparel was of an almost flaring order.

Her large-sleeved bodice of flowered blue silk, snug to the belted waist, suggested Henley rather than the high road out of squalid Lambeth. Her straw sailor-hat, jauntily borne on the primrose fluff and coils of hair, belonged, too, not a mile lower on the river than Teddington. She should by rights have a racquet in her hand, and be moving along over the close-shaved lawn of Kanelagh's park, on a hazy, languid summer afternoon.

What on earth was she doing on Westminster Bridge, at this ridiculous hour, in this dismal company? Then speculation died abruptly. She was close to him now, and he recognized her. She was a young woman whom he had seen in the British Museum reading room a score of times.

Her face was entirely familiar to him. Only the other day he had got down for her, from the county-histories shelves, two ponderous volumes which she had seemed unable to manage by herself. She had thanked him with a glance and a pleasant nod. He seemed to recall in that glance a tacit admission that they were old acquaintances by sight.

He looked her square in the eye, meanwhile, the inner muscles of his face preparing and holding in readiness a smile in case she gave a sign of remembering him. For a moment it appeared that she was passing without recognition. He had the presence of mind to feel that this was a gross and inexcusable mischance. His feet instinctively poised themselves to follow her, as if it were for this, and this only, that they had tarried so long on the bridge.

Before he could take a step, however, she had halted, and, in a wavering fashion, moved sidelong out of the main current of pedestrians. She stood irresolutely by the parapet for a few seconds, with a pretence of being interested in the view of the river and the prim stretch of Parliamentary architecture on its right bank. Then, with a little shrug of decision, she turned to him.

"It is a fine morning," she said.

He had stepped to her side, and he bent upon her now the smile which had so nearly gone a-begging. "I was afraid you hadn't noticed me—and I had quite resolved to go after you."

She flashed inquiry into his face, then let her glance wander vaguely off again. "Oh, I saw you well enough," she confessed, with a curious intermingling of hesitation and boldness; "but at first I wasn't going to pretend I did. In fact, I don't in the least know why I did stop. Or, rather, I do know, but you don't, and you never will. That is to say, I shan't tell you!"

"Oh, but I do know," he answered genially. "How should you imagine me so deficient in discernment? Only—only, I think I won't tell either."

She looked at him again with a kind of startled intentness, and parted her lips as if to speak. He fancied that he caught in this gaze the suggestion of a painful and humbled diffidence. But then she tossed her head with a saucy air and smiled archly.

"What a tremendous secret we shall carry to our graves!" she laughed. "Tell me, do you sleep on the bridge? One hears such remarkable stories, you know, about the readers at the Museum."

He regarded her with pleasure beaming in his eyes. "No, I go entirely without sleep," he replied, with gravity, "and walk about the streets turning a single idea for ever in my mind; and every morning at daybreak—oh, this has gone on for years now—I come here to watch for the beautiful girl with the yellow hair who some time is to come up to me and remark, 'It is a fine morning.' A fortune-teller told me, ever so long ago, that this was what I must do, and I've never had a moment's rest since."

"You must be very tired," she commented, "and a good deal mixed in your mind, too, especially since yellow hair has come so much into fashion. And did the fortune-teller mention what was to happen after the—the beautiful lady had really appeared?"

"Ah, that is another of my secrets!" he cried, delightedly.

They had begun to stroll together toward the clock-tower. The throng bustling heedlessly past with hurried steps gave them an added sense of detachment and companionship. They kept close together by the parapet, their shoulders touching now and again. When they reached the end of the bridge, and paused to look again upon the river prospect, their manner had taken on the ease of people who have known each other for a long time.

The tide was running out now with an exaggerated show of perturbed activity. The girl bent over, and stared at the hurrying current, sweeping along in swirling eddies under the arch, and sucking at the brown-grey masonry of the embankment wall as it passed. Her silence in this posture stretched out over minutes, and he respected it.

At last she had looked her fill and turned, and they resumed their walk. "I could never understand drowning," she remarked, musingly; "it doesn't appeal to me at all, somehow. They talk about its being pleasant after the first minute or so, but I don't believe it. Do you?"

"There might possibly be some point about it—if one could choose the fluid," he replied, achieving flippancy with an effort.

"Like the Duke of Clarence, for example."

"How do you mean? The papers all said it was influenza. Oh, I see—you mean the Shakespeare one." Her good faith was undoubted. "But no, we were speaking of drowning—of suicide."

"No, we weren't," he said, soberly. The memory of his own mood a brief half-hour ago stirred uneasily within him. "And we're not going to, either. What the mischief have you—young and healthy and happy and pretty as a peach—to do with any such things?"

"In fact," she went on thoughtfully, as if he had not spoken, "all kinds of death seem an outrage to me. They make me angry. It is too stupid to have to die. What right have other people to say to me, 'How you must die'? I was born to live just as much as they were, and I have every whit as much right on the earth as they have. And I have a right to what I need to keep me alive, too. That must be so, according to common-sense!"

Mosscrop had listened to this declaration of principles but indifferently. A sense of drowsiness had stolen over him, and, yielding to it for the moment, he had hung his head, with an aimless regard upon the pavement. All at once he caught sight of something that roused him. His companion's little boot, disclosed in movement beneath her skirt, was broken at the side, and almost soleless. He lagged behind for a step or two, and made sure of what he saw. The girl in the silken blouse was shod like a beggar.

"Which way are you going?" he asked, with a pretence of suddenly remembering something. He had halted, and they stood at the corner, looking up Whitehall. He smothered a yawn with a little explanatory laugh. "I made rather a night of it—it's my birthday today—and I'm half asleep. I hadn't noticed where we'd walked to. I hope I haven't taken you out of your way."

The girl hesitated, looked up the broad, stately street, and bit her lip in strenuous thought of some sort.

"Good morning, then!" she blurted out, confusedly, and turned to move away.

The impulse to be quit of her had been very sharply defined in his mind, and had dictated not only his words, but his awkward, half-shamefaced, half-familiar, manner in suggesting a parting. Now it vanished again with miraculous swiftness.

"No, no! You mustn't go off like that!" he urged, and sprang forward to her side. "I only asked you which was your way."

She was blinking her eyes in a struggle to regain facial composure.

He could see that she had been on the point of tears, and the sight moved him to recklessness. It was not surprising to hear her confess: "Me? I have no way."

He took charge of her with a fine paternal tone. "Oh yes, you have! Your way is my way. You are going with me. It's my birthday, you know, and you have come to help me celebrate it. What do you say to beginning with a special breakfast?—or perhaps you've spoiled your appetite already. But you can pretend to eat a little."

The girl laughed aloud, with pathetic irony at some conceit which curled her lip in scornful amusement. Words rose to her tongue, but she forbore to utter them, and stared up the street.

"You'll come along, won't you?" He had held up his hand, and a four-wheeler, with a driver and horse of advanced years and dejected aspect, was crawling diagonally across the roadway toward them.

She took courage to look him frankly in the face. "I shall be very much obliged to you, indeed," she said, keeping her voice up till the avowal should be finished. "I've had no breakfast."

The ancient cab, with a prodigious rattling of framework and windows for its snail's progress, bore them along past Trafalgar Square, and westward through narrow streets, already teeming with a busy, foreign-looking life, till it halted before a restaurant in one of the broader thoroughfares of Soho.

When they had alighted, and the sad old driver, pocketing his shilling in scowling silence, had started off, a thought occurred to Mosscrop.

"I tell you what we'll do," he broke forth. "We'll decree that it's your birthday, too, so that we can celebrate them together. That will be much more fun. And before we go into breakfast, I must get you a little present of some sort, just to mark the occasion. Come, you haven't anything to say about it at all. It's my affair, entirely."

He led the way along past several shops, and halted in front of a narrow window in which a small collection of women's boots was displayed. A man in shirt-sleeves and apron had just taken down the shutter, and stood now in the doorway, regarding them with a mercantile yet kindly smile.

"It is the best Parisian of make," the shoeman affirmed, to help forward Mosscrop's decision.

"You can see how different they are from ordinary English things," said David, argumentatively. "The leather is like a glove, and the workmanship—observe that! I don't believe any lady could have a more unique present than a pair of real French boots."

The girl had come up, and stood close beside him, almost nestling against his shoulder. He saw in the glass the dim reflection of her pleased face, and moved toward the door as if it were all settled. Then, as he stepped on the threshold, she called to him.

"No—please!" she urged. "I think we won't, if you don't mind."

"Of course we will!" he insisted, turning in the doorway. "Why on earth shouldn't we? It's your birthday, you know. Come, child, you mustn't be obstinate; you must be nice, and do what you're told."

As she still hung back, shaking her head, he went out to her. "What's the matter? You liked the idea well enough a minute ago. I saw you smiling in the window there. Come! don't let a mere trifle like this spoil the beginning of our great joint-birthday. It's too bad of you! Won't you really have the boots—from me?"

"Well," she made answer, falteringly, "it's very kind—but if I do, I'd rather you didn't come into the shop—that is, that you went out while I was trying them on—because—well, it is my birthday, you know, and I must have my own way—a little. You will stop outside, won't you?"

This struck him as perhaps an excess of maidenly reserve. He smiled impatiently. "By all means, if it is your whim. But—but I'm bound to say—I suppose different people draw the line at different places, but feet always seemed to me to be relatively blameless things, as things go. Still, of course, if it's your idea."

"No, if you take it that way," she said, "we'll go and get our breakfast, and say no more about it." She found the fortitude to turn away from the window as she spoke.

"If I take it that way!" The perverseness of this trivial tangle annoyed him. "Why, I consented to stop outside, didn't I? What more is demanded? Do you want me to pass a vote of confidence, or shall I whistle during the performance, so that you may know I am cheerful, or what? Suppose I told you that I had been a salesman in a boot-shop myself, and had measured literally thousands of pretty little feet—would that reassure you? I might come in, then, mightn't I?"

"No—you never were that—you are a gentleman." She stole a perplexed glance up at him, and sighed. "I should dearly love the boots—but you won't understand. I don't know how to make you." Looking into his face, and catching there a reflection of her own dubiety, she burst suddenly into laughter.

"You are a gentleman, but you are a goose, too. My stockings are too mournful a patchwork of holes and darning to invite inspection—if you will have it."

"Poor child!" He breathed relief, as if a profoundly menacing misunderstanding had been cleared up. "Here, take this and run across to that fat Jewess in the doorway there. She will fit you out."

Presently she returned, with beaming eyes, and an air of shyness linked with complacent self-approbation which he found delightful.

"Oh, I should simply insist on your coming in now," she cried gaily, at the door of the boot-shop, in answer to his mock look of deferential inquiry.

Chapter 2

There surely was never such another breakfast in the world!

She spoke with frank sincerity. Upon afterthought she added: "I don't believe any woman could order a meal like that. You men always know so much about eating."

Mosscrop leaned back in his chair, crossed his knees, and took a cigar from his pocket. His mind ran in pleasurable retrospect over the dishes—a fragrant omelet with mushrooms, a sole Marguerite, a delicate little steak that had been steeped in oil over night, a pulpy Italian cheese which he never got elsewhere than here. The tall-shouldered, urn-shaped green bottle on the table still held a little Capri, and he poured it into her glass.

"Yes," he assented, "I find myself paying more attention to food as I get older. It is the badge of advancing years. It is a good little restaurant, isn't it? I come here a great deal."

"And that is how you are able to order such wonderful breakfasts for hungry young ladies. It comes of practice. Do they all enjoy it as much as I have?"

"You mustn't ask things like that," he remonstrated, smilingly, as he lit a match. "I hope you don't mind?—thanks."

He regarded her contemplatively through the dissolving haze of the first mouthful of smoke. They had the small upstairs dining-room to themselves, and she, from her seat by the window, let her glances wander from him to the street below, and back again, with a charming, child-like effect of being delighted with everything.

The sight of her opposite him stirred new emotions in his being. He imported a gentle gravity into his smile, and dropped the jesting tone from his voice. "No—we must play that I have never breakfasted with anybody before—like this—either here or anywhere else. Let us both start fresh on our birthday. We wipe everything off the slate, and make a clean beginning. First of all, you haven't told me your name."

"My name is Vestalia Peaussier."

"Then you are not English? I could have sworn you were the most typically English girl I'd ever laid eyes on."

"My father was a French gentleman—an officer, and a man of position. He died—killed in a duel—when I was very young. I do not remember him at all. My mother brought me away from France at once. She was dreadfully crushed, poor lady. She was the daughter of a very old Scottish house—it had been a runaway love match—and her people, my grandparents——"

"What part of Scotland? What was their name? I am a Scot myself, you know."

Vestalia paused briefly, and sipped at her wine. "I was going to say—my grandparents behaved so unfeelingly to my mother that she never permitted herself to mention their name. I do not know it myself. I gathered as a child from poor mother's words that they were extremely wealthy and proud, and had a title in the family. It is not probable that I shall ever learn more. I should not wish to, either, for it was their hard cruelty which broke my mother's heart. She died two years ago. Poor unhappy lady!"

Mosscrop nodded sympathetically. "And were you left without anything?"

"My mother's private fortune had been diminished to almost nothing by bad investments and the treachery of others before her death. I had no one to advise me—I was all alone—and the lawyers and others probably robbed me cruelly. Only a few of her old family jewels were left to me—and one by one I had to part with these. Some of them, I daresay, were of great antiquity and priceless value, if I had only known, but I was forced to sell them for a song.

There were wonderful signet-rings among them, all with the crest of the family—I suppose it must have been her family—and at first I thought of using it to trace them—but then my girlish pride——"

"What was the crest?" asked David. "Perhaps it wouldn't be too late, now."

Again Vestalia hesitated. Then she shook her head. "No; dear mamma's wishes are sacred to me. I do not wish to learn what she thought it best to keep from me."

"Well—and when the jewels were all sold?"

"Long before that I had begun to work for my living. I write a good hand naturally. I got employment as a copyist, but that did not last very long. I was ambitious, and I thought I might work my way into literature. But it is a very disheartening career, you know."

Mosscrop had lifted his brows in some surprise. He nodded again, with a cursory "Ay!"

"The editors were not at all kind to me," she went on. "I toiled like a slave, but I hardly ever got anything accepted, and then you had to wait months for your pay, and perhaps not get it at all. I should have starved long ago, if I hadn't met an American woman at the Museum who was over here getting up pedigrees. Oh, not for herself. She made a regular business of it. Rich Americans paid her to hunt up their English ancestors, in genealogies and old records, and on tombstones and so on. I was her assistant for nearly a year, and things went fairly well with me. But three months ago she was taken ill and had to go home, and there I was stranded again. I tried to go on with some of the jobs she left unfinished, but the people had gone away, or hadn't confidence in so young a person, and well—that's all. My landlady turned me out at six o'clock this morning, and she has seized the few poor things I had left—and here I am."

The young man lifted his glass, and clinked it against hers. "I am very glad that you are here," he said; and they smiled wistfully into each other's eyes as they finished the Capri.

"It is a heavenly little break in the clouds, anyway," she went on, dreamily. "It isn't like real life at all: it is the way things happen in fairy stories."

"Quite so. Why shouldn't we have a fairy story all by ourselves? It is every bit as easy as the stupid, humdrum other thing, and a million times nicer. Oh, I'm on the side of the fairies, myself."

She looked out, in an absent fashion, at the windows across the way. The light began to fade from her countenance, and the troubled lines returned.

"Every day for a fortnight I have been answering advertisements," she went on, pensively; "some by letter, some in person. There were secretaries' places, but you had to know shorthand, and the typewriter, and all that. Then somehow all the vacancies for shop-women got filled before I applied, or else people with experience in the business were preferred to me. I even went in for the 'lady-help' thing—a kind of domestic servant, you know, only you get less pay and don't wear a cap—but nobody would have me. My hair was too good and my boots were too bad. The lady of the house just stared at these two things, every place I applied at, and said she was afraid I wouldn't answer."

The picture she drew was painful to Mosscrop, and he made an effort to lighten it with levity. "I confess I didn't think very highly of your boots, myself," he said, cheerily, "but I admire your hair immensely."

"Oh, but you are a man!"

He chuckled amiably at the implication of her retort, and she laughed a little, too, in a reluctant way. "It occurs to me," he ventured, pausing over his words, "that men seem to have played no part whatever in the story of your life."

"No, absolutely none," she answered, with prompt decision. "I have never before been beholden to a man for so much as a biscuit or a shoe-button. I don't know that you will believe me when I tell you, but I've never even been alone in a room with a man before in my life."

"Of course, I believe what you say. It is remarkably interesting, though. Come! First impressions are the very salt of life. I should dearly like to know what you think of the novel experience, as far as you've gone."

She seemed to take him seriously. Placing her elbows on the table, and poising her chin between thumbs and forefingers, she bestowed a frank scrutiny upon his face, as intent and dispassionate as the gaze which a professor of palmistry fastens upon the lines of the client's hand.

"First of all," she said, deliberately, "I am not so afraid of you as I was."

"Delightful!" he cried. "Then I did inspire terror at the outset. It has been the dream of my life to do that—if only just once. I feared I should never succeed. My dear lady, you have rescued me from my own contempt. My career is not a blank failure after all. We must have coffee and a liqueur after that!"

He pressed the bell at his side. She frowned a little at his merry exuberance.

"I am not joking," she complained. "You asked me to say just what I felt."

He nodded his contrition as the waiter left the room.

"Yes, do," he urged. "I will keep as still as a mouse."

"I am not as afraid of you as I was," she repeated, dogmatically. "But I think, even if I knew you ever so well, I should always be just the least weeny bit afraid. I can see that you are very kind—my Heavens! nobody else has ever been a hundredth part as kind to me as you are—but all the same—yes, there is a but if I can explain it to you—I get a feeling that you are being kind because it affords you yourself pleasure, rather than because it helps me.

No—that is not quite what I mean either. It seems to me that a man will be much kinder than any woman knows how to be, so long as he feels that way; but when he doesn't feel that way any more—well, then he'll chuck the whole thing, and never give it another thought."

"That is very intelligent," said Mosscrop.

He had the appearance of turning it over in his mind, and liking it the more upon consideration. "Yes, that is soundly reasoned. I can well believe your mother was a Scots lass."

Vestalia flushed, no doubt with pride.

"Well, then, hear me out," she said, with a pleasant little assumption of newly-gained authority. "Now, I've hardly known a man to speak to—that is, a gentleman, as a friend, you know—if I'm justified in calling you so on such short acquaintance—or no, I mustn't say that, must I? We are friends—but it's a new experience, quite, to me. As you say, I have my first impression of what it is like to have a man for a friend."

The waiter, pushing the door open with his foot, brought in a tray with white cups and silver pots, and wee tinted glasses, and a tall, shapeless bottle encased in a basket-work covering of straw.

"I ordered maraschino," remarked Mosscrop, as the man poured the coffee. "If you prefer any other, why, of course——"

"Oh no; whatever you say is good, I take with my eyes shut."

She sipped at the little glass he had filled for her, and then, with a movement of lips and tongue, mused upon the unaccustomed taste. An alert glance shot at him from her eyes.

"I hope——" she began to say, and stopped short.

"You hope what?"

"No; I won't say what I was going to. It would have been a very ungrateful speech. Only, you must bear in mind that I hardly know one wine from another, and I am leaving myself absolutely in your hands. You will see to it, won't you, that—that I don't drink more than I ought."

Mosscrop waved his hand in smiling reassurance.

"But now for that famous first impression of yours."

She narrowed her eyelids to look at him, and he found her glance invested with something like tenderness of expression. Her head was tilted a bit to one side, so that the light from the window fell full upon the face.

It was a more beautiful face than he had thought, with exquisitely faint and shell-like gradations of color upon the temples and below the ears, where the strange but lovely primrose hair began.

A soft rose-tint had come into her cheeks, which had seemed pallid an hour before. The whole countenance was rounded and mellowed and beautified in his eyes, as he answered her lingering, approving gaze.

"My impression?" she spoke slowly, and with none of the assurance which had marked her earlier deliverance. "Well, you know, I don't feel as if I knew men any more than I did before. I only know one man—a very, very little. I don't believe that other men are at all like him, or else we should hear about it. The world would be full of it. No one would talk of anything else. But the man I do know—that is, a little—well, I'd rather know him than all the women that ever were born, even if I had to be afraid of him all the while into the bargain."

Mosscrop laughed.

"We did well to label it in advance as a first impression. It is the judgment of a babe just opening its eyes. My dear child, I'm afraid this isn't your birthday, after all. You're clearly not a year old yet."

"You always joke, but I'm in sober earnest." She indeed spoke almost solemnly, and with an impressive fervor in her voice. "You do impress me just like that. I wish you'd believe that I'm saying exactly what I feel. Mind, I expressly said, I don't suppose for a minute that other men are like you."

"No, you're right there," he broke in. Her manner, even more than the speech, affected him curiously. He drained his liqueur at a gulp, stared out of the window, fidgeted on his chair, finally rose to his feet.

"You're right there!" he reiterated, biting his cigar and thrusting his hands deep in his pockets. She would have risen also, but he signed to her to sit still.

"Other men are not like me, and they can thank God that they're not. They know enough to keep sober; I don't. They are of some intelligent use in the world; I'm not. They lead cleanly and decent lives, they control themselves, they make names for themselves, they do things which are of some benefit at least to somebody. Ah-h! You hit the nail on the head. They are different from, me!"

She gazed up at him, dumb with sheer surprise. He took a few aimless steps up and down, halted to scowl out of the window at the signs opposite, and then flung himself into the chair again. Sprawling his elbows on the table, he bent forward and fastened upon her a look of such startled intensity that she trembled under it and drew back.

"Why, do you know, you foolish little girl," he began, in a hoarse, declamatory voice, "that a few minutes before you came along, there on the bridge, I was going to throw myself into the river, because I wasn't fit to live. Do you realize that I had sat in judgment upon myself, and condemned myself to death—death, mind you!—because I was an utterly hopeless creature, a waste product, a drunkard, a sterile fool and loafer, a veritable human swine? That is the truth! Do you know where I spent last night— where I woke up, sick with disgust for myself, this morning? No, you don't; and there's no need that I should tell you."

"I don't care!" The girl's lips propelled the words forth with extraordinary swiftness, but the eyes with which she regarded her companion, and the rest of her face, grown pale once more, remained unmoved.

"No, you don't care!" he groaned out a long sigh, and went on with waning vigor. "But I care! It is something to one that I am what I am; that I have wasted my life, that I have done nothing, and worse than nothing, with my chances, that I——"

"You misunderstand me," Vestalia interposed, with a perturbed simulation of calm. "What I meant was that whatever happened last—that is, at any time before this morning—makes no difference whatever in my—my liking for you." Her eyes brightened at the thought of something.

"It was you yourself who said we would wipe the slate clean, and begin all over again quite fresh. Don't you remember? And we were to have our own fairy story, all to ourselves. You do remember, don't you?"

He still breathed heavily, but the gloom upon his face began to abate as he looked at her. He moved one of his hands forward on the table to the neighborhood of hers, and stroked the cloth gently as if it were her hand he touched. A weary smile, born in his eyes, strengthened and spread to soften his whole countenance.

"Yes, I remember everything," he mused, with a kind of forlorn gladness in his tone. It seemed an invitation to silence, and they sat without words for a little.

With a constrained air of having convinced herself by argument that it was the right thing to do, Vestalia all at once lifted her hand, and laid it lightly on his. He fancied that it trembled a little. His own certainly shook, though he pressed it firmly upon the table.

"Now the bad spirits have all gone," he said; "it is fairyland again."

"Ah, we must keep it so," she answered, and pressed his hand softly before she withdrew her own. The black mood had fled from him as swiftly as it came. Vestalia's eyes beamed at the sight of his restored good-humor with himself, and she nodded gay approbation.

"I fancy we've about exhausted the delights of this place," he remarked, after a brief silence filled for both of them with a pleasantly sufficient sense of friendship at its ease. "I'll pay the bill, and we'll toddle."

She glanced about her. "I shall always remember this dear little stuffy old room. I almost hate to leave it at all. I want to fix in my mind just how it looks."

"Oh, we'll come often again," he remarked, lightly. Then it occurred to him that this assurance contained perhaps an element of rashness. "Have you got anything special to do today?" he asked, with awkward abruptness.

The question puzzled and troubled her. "I was going to celebrate my birthday," she murmured, with a wistful, flickering smile ready to fade into depression.

"Of course you are; that's all settled," he responded, making up by the heartiness of his tone for the forgetful stupidity of his query. "What I meant was—what were you thinking of doing before—before you knew you had a birthday on hand?"

Vestalia examined the bottom of her coffee-cup, and poked at it with the spoon. "Me? Oh, I had several things to do," she made reply, hesitatingly. "I had to find something to eat, and contrive how to earn some money, and hunt up a new lodging, and see how I was going to feed myself tomorrow, and—and other small matters of that sort."

His comment was prefaced with a kind, sad little laugh.

"You must go to the old place, and get your things," he said. "How much do you owe?"

"I'd rather not go back at all." She ventured to look up at him now. "I don't want ever to lay eyes on that old hag again."

"But your things. If I sent a commissionaire, would she give them up?—on payment of the bill, of course."

"They're not worth a bus-fare—they're really not. You see," she went on with her reluctant confidences, "I had to pawn everything. These clothes I have on are every rag I have left."

Mosserop, regarding her with a sympathetic gaze, recalled very clearly the gown she used to wear at the Museum. It was a queer color—a sort of rusty greenish-blue; it was of common stuff, and made without a waist, in some outlandish Grosvenor Gallery fashion novel to his eye. The practical side of him stumbled at this memory.

"But if you had to pawn things," he said, "I should have thought these silks you have on would have gone first. That frock you used to wear at the Museum, for instance—you could only have raised a few pence on that—whereas these things—I'm afraid, my young friend, that you haven't a good business head."

"Oh, better than you think," she retorted, with downcast eyes. Her further words cost her a visible effort. "I thought it all out, and I saw that my only chance was to hang on to these clothes. If people didn't happen to look at my boots, I was all right. Men don't notice such things much—you yourself didn't at first. And my skirt would hide them, more or less."

He looked at her averted face, slowly assimilating the meaning of what she said. Then he hastily turned his chair sidewise, rang the bell for the waiter, lit a fresh cigar, and blew out the match with a sigh which deepened into an audible groan.

"What else could I do?" she faltered, with a flushing cheek, and a tear-dimmed stare out of the window. "Nothing but throw myself into the river. And that I won't do. They have no right to insist upon my doing that. If I was old and horrid, it wouldn't matter so much. But I'm young, and I want to live. That's all I ask —just the chance to live. And that I won't let them rob me of, if I can help it."

The waiter, counting out the change, embraced the couple in a series of calm, sidelong glances. He expressed polite thanks for the shilling pushed aside toward him, and closed the door behind him when he left the room with an emphasized firmness of touch.

Mosscrop rose. "Come, child," he said, briskly. "Cheer up! Look up at me—let's sec a smile on your face. A little brighter, please—that's more like it. How we have wiped the slate clean! We begin absolutely fresh. Dry your eyes, and we'll make a start. We've got those celebrated birthdays of ours to look after—and it's high time we set about it."

She stood up, and smilingly obeyed him by dabbing the napkin against her nose and brows. She moved across to the mirror above the mantel, and smiled again at what she saw. Then she looked down at her boots, and her face took on a radiance, which it kept, as she descended close behind him the narrow stairway.

Chapter 3

There was a bar at the front of the restaurant—a cheerful, domestic bar of the Italian sort, with a bright-eyed, smiling, middle-aged woman in charge. She knew Mosscrop, and flashed a kindly glance of southern comradeship at him as he came forward, and stopped and drew his cheque-book from his pocket.

There were also two girls in the bar, and they knew him too, and grinned gently at his salute. Vestalia watched them narrowly, and fancied that one of them also winked.

"I had to stop and get some more money," he explained, when they were in the street together. "There isn't another place in these parts where they would change a cheque."

"I noticed that they seemed to know you," she replied, with reserve.

"Dear people that they are!" he cried. "The sight of them in the morning is always delightful to me. Did you observe it—the extraordinary cheerfulness of them all? You saw how the girls chaffed the ice-man, and how the fellow who brought in the soda-water cases had his joke with the waiters, and how madame clucked and chuckled like a good hen, as if they were all her brood, and everybody seemed to like everybody else?"

"I didn't get the notion that they were very keen about me," remarked Vestalia. "As a matter of sober fact, they scowled."

"Nonsense! Of course they were deferential to you—you represented a sort of dignified unaccustomedness to them, and they were afraid to beam at you. But bless you, they're as simple and as sweet-hearted as children. They laugh and smile at people just out of pure native amiability. The place is as good as a tonic to me of a morning when I am feeling blue and out of sorts."

"But you are not this morning," she reminded him.

For answer he drew her hand through his arm. They fell into step, and moved along at a sauntering gait on their way toward Oxford Street.

It was mid-August, and there had been a shower overnight. The pavement still showed damp in its crevices, and the air was clear and fresh.

A pale hazy sunshine began to mark out shadows in the narrow thoroughfares. By-and-by it would be hot and malodorous here, but just now the sense of summer's charm found them out even in Soho.

She had asked him about himself. The question had risen naturally enough to her lips, and she had propelled it without diffidence. But when the words actually sounded in her own ears, they frightened her. The inquiry seemed all at once personal to the point of rudeness. The possibility of his resenting her curiosity rose in her mind, and on the instant flared upward into painful certainty.

"Oh, forgive me; I had no business to ask you!" she hurriedly added.

He laughed, and patted her arm. "Why on earth shouldn't you?"

"I spoke without thinking," she faltered. "I suppose—that is, it occurs to me—perhaps gentlemen don't like to be questioned—what I mean is, you didn't answer, and I was afraid——"

"Afraid nothing!" he reassured her. "You mustn't dream of being stand-offish with me. I shall get vexed with you if you do. My dear little lady, there isn't anything in the world that you're not as free as air to say to me, or ask me. I only hesitated because"—he began, smiling in a rueful, whimsical way down at her—"because it's too complicated and sinister a recital to rush lightly into. My name is David Mosscrop, and I am an habitual criminal by profession. That will do to start with."

Vestalia looked earnestly into his face for some sign that he was jesting. It was a clean-shaven face, cast by nature in a mold of gravity. The eyes had seemed a pleasant grey to her first cursory examination; but now, on closer scrutiny, there might be a hardness as of steel in their color.

The lips and chin, too, had a sharpness of line that could mean unamiable things. And yet, how could she credit his words? It was true, she recalled, that by all accounts many superior gamblers, burglars, and other evil characters were in private life most kindly persons—of notoriously generous impulses.

Pictures of the outlaws of romance, from Robin Hood to Dick Ryder, crowded upon her mental vision. The countenance into which she tremulously stared might have belonged to any of them—a little blurred by the effects of recent drink, a trifle stained in its lower parts by the need of a razor, yet adventurous, subtle, courageous; above all, commanding.

Her heart fluttered at the thought of her own temerity in

leaning on his arm, and she shot a swift glance forward toward the big thoroughfare they were nearing, where there would be crowds of people to see her. Then she tightened her hold, and said to herself that she didn't mind a bit.

"You said I might ask anything I liked," she found herself saying. "What is your special line of crime?"

"Well, specifically, I don't know just how they would define me. I am not quite a confidence-man, because nobody ever reposes an atom of confidence in me. Mine is a peculiar sort of case. I cannot be said to deceive any one by my game, and yet, undoubtedly, I come under the general head of impostors. I make my living by obtaining money under false pretences."

The girl was frankly mystified. This sounded so poor and mean that her instincts fluttered back to the original notion that he was joking. Sure enough, she could see the laughter latent in his eyes, now that she looked again.

"You're just fooling!" she protested, and tugged admonishingly upon his arm. "Tell me what it is you do, quick!"

"How do you know I do anything?" he demanded. He hugged her arm against his side, to show what great fun it all was.

"Why shouldn't I be a gentleman at large? There are such things, you know."

She shook her head. "Gentlemen at large don't read hard at the Museum in August. I never understood they were much given to reading at any time of year, for that matter. No, I know you do something. You are in a profession; I can see that. You are not a doctor; you are too polite and kind-mannered for that. I thought at first that you were a journalist, but they don't have cheque-books. Oh, tell me, please!"

He laughed gaily. "Ten thousand guesses and you'd never hit it. My dear lady, I profess Culdees."

Vestalia pondered the information with gravity for a little, stealing sidelong glances to learn if this was more of his fun. "You can see how ignorant I am," she remarked at last. "You will recognize that you are wasting your time with me. What are Culdees? Or is it a thing? I assure you I haven't the remotest notion."

"It is a secret," he assured her, in tones which strove to be serious, but revealed a jocose note to her ear.

She shook his arm gleefully. "As if we could have secrets on our birthday!" she cried. "Tell me instantly all about Culdees! I insist."

"But I don't know anything about them. That is the secret— nobody knows anything about them. I draw a salary for devoting three weeks each year to explaining to a class of young men who desire to know nothing whatever about the Culdees, that if they did wish to learn about them they couldn't possibly do it."

"Are there any more jobs like that, that you know of?" inquired the girl. "It would just suit me." Then she spoke less flippantly. "I'm afraid you've already discovered how shallow and ill-informed I am. You do not think it is worth while to talk seriously with me!"

He seemed much affected by her rebuke. "My dear lady——" he began, in earnest disclaimer.

"No; what I mean is—" she interrupted him—pleased by his show of contrition, but even more interested in the flow of her own ideas, and the sound of her own voice, which had taken on musical intonations, and delicately-measured cadences since breakfast that were novel to her delighted hearing—

"what I mean is, men do not have any real intellectual respect for women; they do not think of them in their deep-down thoughts as their mental equals; they still regard them, as their ancestors did thousands of years ago, as mere toys, playthings, creatures to pat on the cheek and talk pleasant nonsense to, when there is nothing better to do. And the worst of it is that so many women—a large majority—are contented with this, and aspire to nothing higher, and they set the rules for the rest; and hence young women who have ambitions, and do desire to make themselves the equals of men, and set up high ideals of intellectual life, they—they find themselves—find themselves——"

"Find themselves being regarded with much very genuine liking and friendship by those to whom they are good enough to give their company," Mosscrop finished the sentence for her.

He smiled to himself as he pressed her arm still more closely. The girl was not accustomed to drink, and the Capri and maraschino had gone to her tongue. He was pleasantly conscious of their influences himself, and upon second thought he liked his companion all the more for the innocent fearlessness with which she had followed his example.

The charm of the whole experience strengthened its hold upon him. He looked down with tenderness upon her. "Yes, very genuine friendship—and gratitude," he reiterated, with ardor in his low voice.

She did not conceal the enjoyment she had in both look and tone.

"The idea of real companionship is so precious in my eyes," she murmured—"a true communion of minds. There is nothing else in life worth living for. Do you think there can be any real friendship without genuine intellectual respect?"

"Oh, I wouldn't lay too much stress on that myself," he answered, lightly. "I find that the fellows I really like the most— the men that I take the most solid comfort in putting in time with —are tremendous duffers from any intellectual point of view, but of course"—he found himself hastily adding—"that is among men. I have never known anything at all about women friends—that is, of what one may honestly call friends. But I am learning fast. I have reached the point of forming an ideal: she must be tall, with her hat just brushing above my collar. She must have the most wonderful pale yellow hair in the world, and the prettiest face, and new French boots—and——"

"You don't care in the least what kind of a mind she has," put in Vestalia, dolefully.

"Ah, you didn't let me finish. She will have a spirit brave and yet tender, a mind broad and capable yet without arrogance, a temperament attuning itself to each passing mood, sunny, shadowed, merry, pensive, adventurous, timid—all as full of sweet little turns and twists and unexpected things in general as an April day. I don't want her learned: I should hate her to be logical. I like her just as she is: I wouldn't have her changed for the world."

In details the definition perhaps left something to be desired. But its form of presentation brought a flush of satisfaction to Vestalia's cheek. She nestled closer still against his shoulder for a dozen paces or so, and when she drew away then, let him feel that it was because they were at Oxford Street, and for no other reason.

"Oh, the beautiful day!" was all she said.

They turned to the right, and sauntered aimlessly along down the broad pavement, pausing now and again to glance over some tradesman's display, then drifting onward again, close together.

Before a bookseller's window at a corner they made a more considerable halt. Mosscrop scanned the rows of titles minutely, talking as he did so. Thus between comments on the volumes they looked at, and idle remarks on subjects which these suggested, she picked up this further account of her new friend's affairs.

"I told you I was a Scotchman," he said. "I was the son of a factor, a sort of steward over a biggish estate, and I never did anything but go to school from the earliest moment I can remember. It is as if I was born in a class-room, and cradled on a blackboard. It is a terrible land for that; tuition broods over it like a pestilence. Their idea is to make of each child's brain a sort of intellectual haggis; the more different kinds of stuff there are in it, the greater the fame of the teacher and the pride of the parents. I shudder now when I think how much I knew at the age of twelve.

As for my eighteenth year, when I took the Strathbogie exhibition, Confucius, John Knox, and Lord Bacon rolled in one would have been frightened of me. My information was appalling. My mother died from sheer excess of astonishment at having given birth to such a prodigy. My father took to drink. The magnificence of my attainments not only threw him off his balance—it debauched the entire district. It is the law of history, you know, that communities and nations progress to a certain point, achieve some crowning deed in a golden age of splendid productiveness, and then wither and go off to seed. Well, my parish, having produced me, reached its climax. Industry flagged, enterprise died down; the very land ceased to grow as much corn to the acre as formerly. The people could do nothing but congregate at the taverns and discuss with bated breath my meteoric progress across the academic heavens. Oh, I was a most remarkable young man!

It happened that there was also a remarkable old man in my neighborhood. He came from nobody in particular, and went away young. People had long since forgotten that there had been such a lad, when one day he returned to us, well along in years, and infamously rich. I don't mean that he had come wrongfully by his money. God knows how he got it; the story ran that it had something to do with smoked fish. Whatever its source, his wealth was wanton, preposterous, criminal in its dimensions. He had no kith or kin remaining to him. Of course we knew he would build and endow an educational establishment. All rich old Scotchmen do that, as an ordinary matter. They have reared for us such myriads of brand-new colleges and seminaries on every hillside that I marvel even the rabbits and pheasants can escape learning to spell. There are logarithms in the very atmosphere.

But this old man was not to be put off with a mere academy. He piled up a veritable castle of instruction, a first-class fortress of learning. And he had an idea of something which should be unique among all the schools of the world. It was all his own idea. Even in Scotland it had not occurred to anyone else. You must know that in early Scotch ecclesiastical history, say from the eighth to the twelfth centuries, there are occasional mentions of some bounders called Culdees, who seem to have run a little sacerdotal show of their own, something between hermits and canons-regular—it is absolutely impossible now to make out just what they were. But this extraordinary old man was quite clear in his mind about them. He had reasoned it all out for himself. He said that 'Culdees' was, of course, a mere popular corruption of 'Chaldees.' He loved to argue this with all comers, and he did so, —my word for it, he did! How nobody in Scotland ever agrees with any view or opinion advanced by any other person, but the art of disagreeing has been reduced, by ages of use, to a delicately-modulated system.

Everybody disputed his ridiculous notion of the 'Chaldees'— they would have fought it just as stoutly if it had been a wise one —but he was a very rich man, and he had benevolent intentions toward the district, and so they 'roared him gently as any sucking dove.' They couldn't admit his contention, oh no, but they let him feel that they were thinking about it, that it had made an impression on their minds, that in due time they might see it differently.

The upshot was that the old fool established a Culdee Chair in the faculty of his new college, and made it worth more money than any other professorship of the lot. The celebrity of my performances at school was fresh then, and reached his ears. He gave the billet to me, and confirmed it to me in his will when he died, a year later—and that is all."

"And you actually only work three weeks a year? And get paid a whole year's salary for that?"

Vestalia regarded him with astonishment, as she put the question.

They had strolled meanwhile down the great thoroughfare, crossed it, and passed into a narrower lateral by-way.

"It is hardly even three full weeks' work," he replied. "There is nothing to do in the way of fresh discovery. Reeves and Skene and other fellows have gleaned the last spear of straw in the stubble. I do go through the form of getting up some lectures each Autumn, but it is really such dreadful humbug that I'm ashamed to look the students in the face, let alone my fellow-professors. Fortunately, most of the latter are clergymen, and that makes it a little easier. They know that they are as big frauds as I am, in their own line of goods, and so we say nothing about it."

"What struck me," she began, hesitatingly, "you spoke rather —what I mean is, you don't appear to be very grateful to the old gentleman who arranged all this for you—and to me it seems the most wonderful thing I ever heard of. I should thank his memory on my bended knees every day of my life if I were the Professor of

Culdees. I couldn't find it in my heart to poke fun at him; I should think of him and revere him as my benefactor, always!"

"Hm—m!" said Mosscrop. "I'm not sure I don't wish he'd never been born, or had choked on a bone of one of his own damned Finnan baddies, before ever he came back to us!"

The ring in his voice, like a surly rattling of chains, brought back to her vividly the scene of his despondency at the restaurant.

She made haste to lay her hand upon his arm.

"Oh, do you see where we are?" she cried, vivaciously, snatching at the chance of diversion.

Sure enough, a section of the Museum's stately front lay before them, filling to topheaviness the perspective of the small street. They had wandered instinctively toward this prenatal rendezvous of their friendship. Their eyes softened now as they looked at the grey, pillared block of masonry stretching across the end of their by-way.

"It draws us like a magnet," said Mosscrop. "Come, what do you say? Shall we go in for an hour, and wander about as if we were nice rural people come up to London to see the sights? I should like to myself."

"The dear old place!" sighed Vestalia, with mellow tones.

Chapter 4

It was a long hour that the Museum claimed from them.

"This is what always attracts me most of all," said Mosscrop upon entering. He turned to the left, and led the way into the little gallery of the Roman portrait-busts. "Very often I never go any farther than this. The modernness of these fellows is a perpetual marvel to me. It is as if we met them every day. Look at Caracalla and Septimius Severus; they are exactly like Irish members. And see Pertinax, here; I know at least ten old farmers about Elgin who might be his own brothers. Observe this man Hadrian. He is the absolute image of Francis the First. You know the portraits of him at Hampton Court—what? never been there? Ah, that's a place we will go to together. There is one picture of Francis there —he is very drunk, apparently, and has got hold of the hand of the Duchess of Some-thing-or-other, and she is in her cups, too, and the inane, leering, almost simian happiness of the two—oh, it is worth a long journey just to see that one picture."

"It doesn't sound very inviting," commented Vestalia. "Tipsy women are repulsive, whether they are duchesses or not."

Mosscrop chuckled. "Oh, but you must make allowances for the period. It was the Renaissance, the joyful, exuberant, devil-may-care Renaissance. If once you catch the inner spirit of it, you will feel that it was the most glorious of periods. And Francis the First was the living, breathing type of it. There was a man for you! He celebrated his birthday all the year round. And in this particular instance, why, I daresay it was the Duchess's birthday too. I should have thought you would take a more lenient view of such a pleasing double anniversary."

Vestalia looked doubtfully at him. "I hope you don't mean that I am in my cups, as you call it," she said.

He laughed her suspicion down. "No, I won't let you hint at such an absurd thing. My dear friend, I must cultivate your sense of humor. The roots exist, but the growth is choked by the weeds of Lambeth—or was it Kennington? We must have them up."

"But I don't know when you are joking," she protested. "Besides, I always understood that the Scotch were not a joking people."

"Ah, you confuse two things. It is said of us, with some justice, that we are slow to comprehend the jokes of others. But of the making of jokes by ourselves there is no end. And—ah, here is Nero. I love Nero!"

"Is that a joke, too?"

"Ah, no," he answered, more seriously. "It is in my nature to love all the people whom history has picked out to condemn. If you knew the sort of creatures who wrote the histories—the old chronicles and records and so on—you would understand my point of view. They were full of all meanness and narrow bigotries; they calumniated everybody they couldn't blackmail. Take the case of Richard Lionheart and his brother John, in your own English history. The former was a ferocious and turbulent blackguard, who neglected all his duties of kingship without shame, plundered his own subjects by torture and rapine, and was altogether a curse to his own people and everybody else. The mere trick of his having a taste for songs and music saved him. He buttered up the bards, and they fastened him in history as a hero. It is precisely the same thing that is done now by politicians who take pains to make friends with the newspapers. On the other hand, John was a model monarch, diligent, hardworking, extraordinarily attentive to his duties, traveling for ever up and down the country to hold courts of justice, and right the wrongs poor people suffered at the hands of the barons and the abbots and other powerful ruffians. It is plain enough that the poor people loved him; after all these centuries his name continues to be the most popular baptismal name among them. But the bards and monkish chroniclers were in the pay of the barons and abbots, and they paint John for us as the most evil scoundrel in English history. That's the way it has always been done. I should like to have Nero's side of his story. I know he must have been a splendid fellow, to have got the historians so violently against him. I shouldn't be surprised if he was really almost as fine as Richard the Third."

"How amusing!" said Vestalia at this point, and Mosscrop was swift to take the hint. They moved on through the Greek rooms, where the girl had more of a chance. She had known a few of the students who are accustomed on giving days to offer up sacrifices of time and crayons and good white paper in front of the more fashionable statues, and this had provided her with what seemed to her companion an exhaustive familiarity with Hellenic art. This advantage followed and remained with her amid the somber and lofty fragments of the Mausoleum, and shone about her when they confronted the frieze of the Parthenon.

"It is not my subject," he remarked, delightedly. "This is a Hermes, you say, and that a Winged Goddess of Victory. Ah, and this is a River God. I don't think I've ever been here before. It is charming—to come with you. We supplement each other. Sure enough, I ought to have foreseen that you would know about Greek art. It is just the field that would attract a beautiful young woman. It fits you—it belongs to you."

"How—now!" she admonished him, holding up a finger in playful protest.

"Oh," he urged, "if I'm not to say that you are beautiful, we might as well not have any birthday at all. That is its most elementary fact—lying at the very foundation of everything. To ignore it would be like trying to celebrate the Fifth of November without a guy."

Again she shot a glance of dubiety at him. "I don't know in the least how to take that," she confessed, with a quiver on her lip.

He laughed outright at this, and gaily patted her on the shoulder. "This unnatural Attic levity of mine is all the fault of the frieze. I'm a cat in a strange garret here. Hasten with me to the Assyrian rooms, if you want to see the utmost height of solemnity it is given to mortals to attain."

He was not quite as good as his word, when they began loitering along before the carved tablets from Nineveh and Khorsabad. Instruction he could not help piling upon his companion, for this was his subject, but he found himself seasoning it with all sorts of sprightly commentaries on the serious text. Of grave and sportive alike he had so much to say that Vestalia took his arm, and leaned upon it as they made their slow progress through the long corridors. The contact was exhilarating to him. He could not be sure that she was assimilating any large proportion of his discourse, but her pretence of interest at least was very pretty, and the touch of her arm in his was full of inspiration to his tongue.

Down in the basement, or crypt, he stood before the lions of Assurbanipal, and talked at length. She said she had read Byron's "Sardanapalus," and he told her how those detestable linguists, the Greeks, had altered the name, and how the Assyrian legends of a great warrior and sovereign had become twisted in the Hellenic after-version to depict a sublimation of debauched effeminacy and luxury run mad. She listened with her shoulder against his—but now he had other auditors as well.

"Excuse me, sir," the urgent and anxious voice of a stranger said close behind him, "but you seem to be extraordinarily well posted indeed on these sculptures here. I hope you will not object to my daughter and me standing where we can hear your remarks."

Mosscrop turned, and saw before him an elderly man, with a mild expression, and hair and beard of extreme whiteness. He was soberly attired, and carried in his hand a broad-brimmed hat of woven white straw. He bowed courteously, and indicated by a gentle gesture the young lady standing at his side.

"I should delight, sir, to have my daughter be privileged to profit by your remarks," he repeated, and bowed again.

The daughter was a dark, well-rounded girl, dressed with much elegance. Her face was strikingly Oriental in type, with coal-black tresses drawn low over the temples, and a skin of a uniform ivory hue. She said nothing, but looked at Vestalia's hair.

Mosscrop spoke somewhat abruptly. "You are certainly welcome, but it happens that I have finished my remarks, as you call them."

"That is too bad," replied the stranger, with a sigh of resignation. "I overheard enough to convince me that they were first-rate. It is our misfortune, sir, mine and my daughter's, to have arrived too late. I presume, sir, that you have given special attention to this branch of study?"

The Professor of Culdees nodded briefly.

"And may I take the liberty of inquiring, sir," the old man persisted, "whether you are professionally engaged in transmitting to others the knowledge which you have thus acquired?"

A stormy grin began twitching at the corners of Mosscrop's mouth. He nodded again.

"My purpose in putting the question is not one of idle curiosity, sir," the other went on. "My life-long desire to visit Europe, and behold its venerable ruins and its remarkable accumulations of objects of historical and artistic interest, has attained fulfillment at a period, unfortunately, when the burden of my years, while not incapacitating me from the enjoyments of the mind, renders me less capable of searching out new information than I should once have been. It also, I see only too clearly, unfits me to act as a guide and interpreter, amid these treasures of the storied past, to a young mind so much fresher and more eager than my own. I recognize this, sir, frankly, and I should be glad to discuss some possible arrangement, with the proper persons, by which my deficiencies might be supplied in this connection."

The elaborate and deferential courtesy with which the old gentleman spoke made a curt answer impossible. Mosscrop looked from father to daughter with a puzzled smile.

"You are Americans, I take it?"

"We are from Paris, sir." He made haste to add, "From Paris, Kentucky. I obtrude the explanation, because I find that among foreigners there is frequently a tendency to confuse our city with the celebrated metropolis on the Continent, which bears the same name, but is a place of an entirely different character. To a scholar like yourself, however, I might have realized that such an error would be impossible. I ask your pardon, sir."

"Oh, don't mention it," replied Mosscrop, lightly. He could not recall ever having heard of such a place before, and for a moment was tempted to say so. But there was an effect of sweet simplicity in the old man's face and manner which restrained his tongue. "Well," he said instead, "what is it that you wish? I am not sure that I have entirely caught your idea. Do you want some one to go round with you and show you things?"

"Not in the ordinary meaning which would attach to that description," the other answered. "We do not require to have things shown to us in the literal sense of the word, but I had thought that if we were attended in our inspection of the various objects of interest for which Europe is justly famous, by some person of erudition and also of an exceptional style of delivery, the experience would be of much greater practical value to my daughter. Of course, sir, I am aware that professional assistance of this high character is not to be obtained without commensurate compensation, but that is a consideration which presents no obstacles to my mind."

David felt Vestalia's hand trembling upon his arm.

"I can see," he said, more amiably, "that such a relation might be extremely welcome to many deserving and very capable men. But at the moment I regret to say I can think of none to recommend to you. Besides, you don't know me from Adam; so how could I give a character to any one else?"

"I beg your pardon sir," rejoined the old gentleman, "but we took the liberty of following close behind you all through the last two long hallways. You were apparently so engrossed with your subject that our proximity escaped your attention, but we have listened with the deepest interest, and I may say improvement as well, to everything which has fallen from your lips. I have thus, sir, been able to form an estimate of your individual characteristics not less than of your acquirements.

I may add, sir, that I am especially impressed by the fact that my daughter, from first to last, displayed an exceptional eagerness to miss nothing of your discourse. As the principal object of my visit to Europe, as, indeed, of my whole existence, is to provide the highest forms of intellectual pleasure and edification for my daughter, I cannot close my eyes to the discovery that your remarks upon Assyrian history produced a much more profound impression upon her young mind than anything which it has been within the scope of my own diminishing powers to produce for her consideration. I have rarely seen her so absorbed, even at our best lectures."

David stifled a yawn, and made a little bow in which, as he turned, he strove to include the young American lady whoso culture was the object of so much solicitude. His movement surprised upon her countenance an expression of scornful weariness, which seemed to render the whole face alert and luminous with feeling. At sight of his eyes, her sultana-like features composed themselves again to an almost stolid tranquility. She regarded him with indolence for an instant, then looked calmly away at things in general. There was to be read in that transient glance a challenge which stirred his blood.

"Well, what you say is, beyond doubt, flattering," he remarked to the father, in a slightly altered voice. "It might be that—that I could find some one for you."

The old gentleman bowed ceremoniously. "Permit me to say, sir, that I have found the some one—a person possessing unique qualifications for the position which I have outlined. I need nothing now but the power to influence his decision in a manner favorable to my aspirations." He turned to Vestalia. "I am emboldened, madame, to crave your assistance in reconciling your husband to my project."

Vestalia's hand fluttered sharply on David's arm, and she parted her lips to speak. At the moment, there was audible a derisive sniff from the daughter.

"It is my rule never to interfere," Vestalia answered with sudden decision, and in a coldly distinct voice. "He is quite capable of settling such matters for himself." She looked from father to daughter and back with an impressive eye.

Mosscrop laughed uneasily. "Well—I'm afraid you must take it that this is settled—I scarcely see my way to avail myself of your very complimentary offer."

The American caught the note of hesitation in his voice. "Perhaps you will turn it over in your mind," he said, fumbling with a hand in his inner breast-pocket. "Allow me, sir, to hand you my card. Adele, you have a pencil? Thank you. I will inscribe upon it the name of the hotel at which we are residing."

Mosscrop took the card, glanced at it, and nodded. "In the extremely improbable event of my changing my mind, I will let you know," he said. "Good day."

As they were parting, the father seemed to read in the daughter's eye that he was forgetting something. He hesitated for a brief space; then his kindly face brightened. "Excuse me, sir," he observed, "but I have neglected to inform myself as to your identity—if I may presume to that extent."

David felt vainly in his pocket. "I haven't a card with me. My name is David Mosscrop. The Barbary Club will find me. I will write it for you."

The old man scrutinized the scrawl in his note-book, and then, after more bows, led his daughter away. She walked after him in a proudly indifferent fashion, with her head in the air, and something almost like a swagger in the movements of her form.

Mosscrop watched them with a ruminating eye till they had left the room. Then he glanced at the card, and gave a little laugh. "Mr. Laban Skinner, Paris, Kentucky.—Savoy Hotel," he read aloud.

"Skinner? Is their name Skinner?" demanded Vestalia with eagerness.

"None other. Why? It's a good name for them, isn't it?"

"Oh yes—good enough," the girl replied, speaking now with exaggerated nonchalance.

"Quaint people these Americans are!" commented Mosscrop. "If I were to put that old chap's speeches down literally in a book nobody would credit them. Fancy the fate of a young woman condemned to be dragged around the globe chained to a preposterous old phonograph like that! It really wrings one's heart to think of it. Mighty good-looking girl too."

Vestalia withdrew her arm. "Perhaps," she said, icily, "if you were to make haste you might overtake them. I must insist on your not allowing me to detain you, if you are so interested. I shall do quite well by myself." Mosscrop gathered her meaning slowly, after a grave scrutiny of her flushed and perturbed face. When it came to him, he shouted his merriment. A glance around the chamber showed him that they were alone with the lions and carved effigies of Sardanapalus.

He thrust an arm about Vestalia's waist, and gave it a boisterous though fleeting squeeze.

"Why, you dear little canary-bird of a creature, do you suppose I've been forgetting you?" he cried. "Haven't I been thinking every minute of the touch of your arm in mine? Haven't I been cursing that old windbag ceaselessly because he was interrupting our birthday? Look up at me! Truly now, aren't you ashamed?"

She suffered him to raise her face, his finger under her chin, and she made a brave effort to smile hack at the glance he bent upon her. "If it is truly—oh, ever so truly—still our birthday—the same as it was before," she made wistful answer.

"It is a hundred times more our birthday than ever!" he protested stoutly.

"Well then," whispered Vestalia, "let's go somewhere else to celebrate the rest of it. All these stone animals and images and mummies—I don't feel as if they brought me luck on my birthday."

So they wandered forth into the sunshine again, and Mosscrop confessed himself glad of the change. Where should they go? He found himself empty of suggestion. Responsibility for the decorous entertainment of a young lady in the daytime was a novel experience, and he said so.

"Oh, let us just stroll about," she urged. "I love these old Bloomsbury Squares. They are so stupid."

Luncheon hour came, and presented itself to Mosscrop as a welcome pretext to take a hansom. A certain formless apprehension of meeting some one he knew—though why this should be dreaded he could not for the life of him have told—had alloyed the pleasure of his ramble. They drove to another restaurant, this time a larger place in a more pretentious quarter —and though they had a little table to themselves, the room was full of others.

David knew about luncheons as well as breakfasts. He gave the waiter very minute instructions about having a grouse split and grilled, and he ran his eye over the list of champagnes with the confident discrimination of an expert. "I will give that number 34a one more trial," he said to the butler. "Cool it to 48, and we will see what it is like then."

Vestalia noted that he spoke to waiters in a soft, grave tone, with shades of gentle melancholy and of affectionate authority subtly blended in it, which he used to no one else. He produced the impression upon her of being at his very best at a table. She particularly liked him when he took the cork from the butler, and tenderly pinched with thumb and finger as he scrutinized it, and then smiled courteous approbation to the servant. This person wore a chain round his neck, and the bottle he brought was swathed in starched napery—and the girl observed both with the interest that attaches to novelty. But it was even more interesting to see how perfectly her companion presided over everything.

She herself was much less at ease. David noticed that she kept her hands in her lap under the table as much as possible during the meal, and that there was an air of constraint in her general deportment which had been lacking at breakfast. He put it down to her shyness among so many busy people in the thronged apartment, and talked briskly at intervals to reassure her. Especially he charged himself with the duty of keeping her glass filled, and he was almost peremptory in his tone with her about the grouse. She ate her piece to the end with meek resolution after that.

When they were again in the open, he rallied her upon the diffidence she had displayed. "You mustn't mind a lot of fellows being about," he said in a paternal way. "They go where there is the best kitchen, and it's the part of wisdom to go there too; besides, they're only too pleased to see a pretty face among them. Didn't you feel how proud I was of you, all the while?"

Outside she had quite regained her spirits and assurance. She smiled with frank gaiety at him. "I'll tell you how to be prouder still," she said. "I know you won't mind my saying so—but I ought really to have some gloves."

"I'm a brute not to have thought of it," Mosscrop reproached himself. "Here's a place, just at hand. I can come in, this time, I suppose, without question."

She held up a finger at him, in mock monition. Then, as they turned to enter the shop, she whispered: "I saw that American girl looking with all her eyes at my bare hands."

"Oh, pshaw—lots of women don't wear gloves. You mustn't be so suspicious of everybody that looks your way. A hundred to one they're thinking about themselves all the time."

"Ah, but you don't know women," she halted midway in the entrance to murmur. "I could read it in her eyes that she'd noticed I had no ring."

"Well, and there too," protested Mosscrop, "you exaggerate the importance of the thing. Lots of women don't wear rings, either— that is, on ordinary occasions."

She danced her eyes at him in merriment. "Perhaps you didn't notice that I was supposed to be a married lady," she said, and then turned abruptly to the counter.

Chapter 5

Ah me! Even the longest and happiest day must have an ending!" sighed Vestalia.

"It is not a new thought," replied David. "But I have never before comprehended how unwelcome it could make itself."

They spoke to each other in soft, regretful, musing tones, through the still darkness of the clouded summer night. They had been the last to quit the Greenwich boat, on its last return to its City moorings, and they halted for a moment on the floating pier after the others had gone—the gentle undulation of the tide beneath their feet, their gaze dwelling upon the black silent expanse of the river.

In retrospect, the day had been very long indeed, and altogether happy. Its structure of delight had been reared on the simplest and most innocent of foundations.

They had gone first to the Zoological Garden, which fortuitously suggested itself to Mosscrop's mental search as an unexceptional resource. Nor did inspiration fail him there, for when the great man-eating cats had been fed, and the foul hyenas next door had yelped themselves hoarse, and the charms of natural history had otherwise begun to wane, the notable thought of the fish dinner at Greenwich rose with splendid opportuneness in his mind.

It was after this feast, while the two strolled beneath the big trees, that twilight found them out. The shadows, as they deepened among the distant shipping, and stole downward to dim the reflected whiteness of the eastern sky beyond the river, brought reverie in their train.

Mosscrop found a bitter taste in his cigar, and lit another impatiently. The girl leaned upon his arm with a new suggestion of dependence.

They moved down to the wharf by tacit consent, before the appointed time, and, taking their seat on a bench at the end, looked absently at the water with but an occasional word.

Evening closed in about them as they sat thus. Then the boat came, and they went on board, and established themselves in relative seclusion at the stern, still in almost unbroken silence.

And now the completed journey lay behind them as well. They stood close together, swaying with the slight motion of the raft upon the lapping waters, and ruminating sadly upon the fact that their day was done.

"We finish as we began—with the river," murmured Vestalia. She trembled to his touch as she spoke.

"Do you remember Henley's lines," said David, meditatively—:

"'The smell of ships (that earnest of romance),
A sense of space and water, and thereby
A lamplit bridge touching the troubled sky,
And look, O look! a tangle of silvery gleams,
And dusky lights, our River and all his dreams,
His dreams of a dead past that cannot die.'"

"No, it cannot die," said Vestalia, slowly. "But its burial time is close at hand, none the less. Ah, the beautiful day!"

They turned and paced up the ascent, and then through obscure, deserted thoroughfares made their way at length to the open space about St. Paul's. The clouds had parted, and the great dome loomed in immensity against a straggling light from the sky. They paused to look at it, and while they stood the fleecy mists far overhead cleared away, and the round moon's full radiance flooded the prospect. Mosscrop gazed up at the flaring satellite, then down at his companion. A new thought sparkled in his eyes.

"And ah, the beautiful tomorrow, too!" he said, confidently. "My good child, do you conceive that the world comes to an end when the sun goes down? Am I less your friend by moonlight than I was in the daytime? Are we changed by the fact that the lamps are lit?"

Vestalia turned her face into the shadow, and said nothing. Mosscrop felt her deep breathing against his arm.

"You have been very dutiful and obedient all day," he began, as they moved along toward Ludgate Hill. "I repudiate the suggestion that you are capable of mutiny now.

Let us speak plainly, dear little lady. How can you suppose that, having watched over you all day and gladly made myself responsible for your well-being since before breakfast, I could wash my hands of you now, and calmly say 'goodbye' at a street corner?"

"You have been very very kind," faltered Vestalia.

"And for that reason it follows that I should be very callous and brutal now, does it? I don't see the logic myself."

"I haven't meant that at all," she interposed in a low voice. She bent her head so that Mosserop could not see her face.

"We will develop and analyze your meanings at our leisure," he said, with a note of authority. "It is more important for the moment to make clear what I mean. The facts are simplicity itself. You have no home, no belongings, no place to sleep, no knowledge of where the morning's breakfast is to come from. You are a beautiful girl, and it is true our civilization is so arranged that beautiful girls rarely starve to death. I do not recall having heard of a single instance, for that matter. But your position makes an imperative demand for assistance from somebody. It cried aloud for help at an early hour this morning. It happened that the appeal was heard and answered. If we were superstitious, we should call it providential."

"Oh, but I do!" protested the girl.

"Very well, then, we are superstitious, and it was providential. These things are governed, I am informed, by immutable laws. Ergo, it is still providential. Who are we, that we should fly in the face of Providence? I adjure you to put away such impious thoughts!"

A little sobbing catch of the breath was her only answer. He divined that there were tears in her eyes, and slowed his pace as they walked along in the gloom of the deserted descent.

At the bottom, under the bridge, the sparkling lights of Fleet Street recalled to him that shops were still open.

"I mentioned that you had no belongings," he resumed, after they had traversed the Circus in silence. "There are little odds and ends of things that you want—the necessities of the toilet, et cetera. Here is a shop; take this sovereign and get the bits of haberdashery that occur to you—such as a lady would put in her dressing-bag if she were to stop overnight in the country. I will go across the way and get the bag itself, and come back for you."

He performed his part of the enterprise with an almost childlike delight. Ladies' dressing-bags cost more than he had imagined, but the shopkeeper said he would take a cheque.

David found something to his mind—a dainty yet capacious trifle, with pretty silver flasks ranged on one side, and a surprisingly comprehensive collection of small implements— scissors, curling-tongs, a manicure set, and other tools the significance of which he could not even guess—packed about in quaint little pockets and crevices.

The outer leather was rich to the eye and delicate to the touch.

A few doors away shone the symbolical red and blue lights of a chemist. Hurrying there, he flung himself eagerly into the task of buying fluids to fill those imposing flasks. The shopkeeper advised him, at first coldly, then with rising enthusiasm.

The best perfumes and vinaigres were expensive, certainly, but then they were the best, and would vouch for themselves to any cultivated feminine mind. There were recondite soaps, and cosmetics to thrill any gentle heart. And in the matter of brushes —here were some silver-backed, and the comb also—to match the flasks. So the list was filled out, and David wrote another cheque with a proud smile.

Vestalia stood at the door of the shop, waiting with a small paper parcel in her hands. Mosscrop was disappointed at its size, and thrust it into the bag with a disdainful shove. They strolled on up the street, and he looked into every lighted window with a hopeful eye. The display of mere masculine or neutral wares affronted him. The shopping fantasy possessed his soul.

"But you really ought to have them. You're not behaving nicely to me in continually saying 'no,'" he urged more than once, as the pressure of his companion's arm drew him away from the tempting windows. She did consent at last to the purchase of some slippers—and he saw to it that they were the choicest that the shelves afforded—soft, luxurious little things, with satin linings and buckles of mother-of-pearl. When these went into the bag, it was filled. He recognized the fact with a regretful sigh.

The creaking old clock-machinery in the belfry of St. Clement Danes set itself in motion as they passed, and the ancient chimes clanged out the full hour. It was nine o'clock.

"I had some thought of a music-hall," he remarked. "But we've had a pretty full day—and a long day, too. I know you must be tired."

"Perhaps—just a little," she answered, softly.

"Then we'll go home," he said, with decision.

It was not a part of London which Vestalia knew very well. Mosscrop led her along the Strand for a little way, then crossed and went up a side street, then turned into a still narrower by-way. The ragged loungers on the walk had an evil aspect, and almost every building seemed to be a public-house. At the last corner a piano-organ of unusual volume shook the air with deafening mechanical din. The man turned the crank so fast, and the dancing children in the radiance from the open-doored tavern on the pavement raised such a racket of their own, that she could barely distinguish the movement of the vulgar tune.

On the borders of darkness beyond were discernible still other children, playing noisily about at the base of groups of fat women in fog-colored shawls and white aprons. Over all the tumult and squalid clustering of humanity there brooded the acrid, musty stench of an antique mid-London slum.

The two turned under an archway, and as by magic the atmosphere freshened and the hubbub ceased. A small square of venerable buildings disclosed itself vaguely in the uncertain light from the sky. Here and there a lamp behind some curtained window made a dim break in the obscurity.

The faint sweet moaning of a 'cello rose from somewhere at the farther end of the space. A stout man with a gold band upon his tall hat revealed himself for a noiseless moment, lifted his finger in salute to Mosscrop, and melted away again into the shadows. Whether they had passed him, or he them, Vestalia could hardly tell. It was all very strange—and a little somber.

A streak of moonlight glanced down between shifting clouds, and fell across the fronts of the houses opposite. There were pale grey tablets of ornamentation set into their mass of dusky brickwork, which looked like tombstones. The girl trembled, and hung back upon Mosscrop's arm as if to halt.

Suddenly, after a brief preliminary scale of piano notes, a woman's clear, practiced voice fell upon the silence in a song—a grave and simple melody full of tenderness. They paused to listen for an instant, and Vestalia traced the sound to an illuminated upper floor at the end of the square.

"Then people live here!" she said, with hesitating re-assurance in her voice.

"Bless you, yes," replied David. "We live here, among others."

He entered the open doorway of the house next to that before which they had paused. The hall was lighted by a single gas-jet at the rear, which only deepened the darkness of the narrow staircase up which he led the way.

It was a very ancient and rickety staircase, with steps worn into queer bumps and hollows by generations of feet. There was not room for her to walk abreast of her guide. He strode ahead, striking matches on the wall as he went. She followed him timorously up the winding ascent, noting the rows of names painted on the big closed doors of each landing they passed.

Mosscrop stopped only when the stairs came to an end. He put down the bag, and she heard the rattle of a key in a lock. Then a match was struck, and a sudden flare of gas lit up the small square hall-way they stood in.

As he pushed open a door to the left, he turned with a smiling face towards his companion. He discovered her drawn back at the edge of the stairs, her hands pressed against her bosom. Her eyes were fastened on him with a troubled look, and the sound of her breathing, quick and labored, reached his ears.

"These stairs are the very deuce when you're not used to them," he said, pleasantly. "I oughtn't to have rushed you up them at such a pace."

"That doesn't matter," panted the girl. "It is I who mightn't to have come up at all."

David's smile deepened and mellowed as he regarded her. "My dear Vestalia," he began, laying a slight and kindly stress upon this first use of her name, "you speak hastily. You must offer no further remarks until you have quite recovered your breath. I will employ the interval by calling your attention to the inscription on the closed door, there, opposite to mine. You will observe that it is 'Mr. Linkhaw.' Have you ever heard it before?"

She shook her head.

"And are you conscious of no novel emotions at hearing it now? Does not the sight of those painted letters cause you to thrill with strange and mysterious sensations? No? What becomes then of the boasted intuition of the feminine mind?"

There seemed to be a jest hidden somewhere in all this, and she smiled plaintively, dubiously. She took her hand from her breast, to show that her breathing was calmer.

"You really assure me," he went on, with a twinkling eye, "that the spectacle of this particular sported-oak does not especially stir your pulses, and peculiarly impress your imagination?"

"Why should it?"

"Why indeed! Ah, young woman, your sex gets much credit that it ill deserves. A mere man could do no worse in the matter of instinct. My dear friend, behind that door lies your present abode. That name 'Linkhaw' is the sign of your home—and you looked at them both and never guessed it!"

Vestalia did not so much as glance at the door in question, but she gazed with much intentness at Mosscrop. "I don't understand—what it is all about?" she said, slowly. He had stepped inside his own door, lighted the gas and pulled down the blinds. He returned, and stretched out his hand to take hers. "Do me the honor to come in and sit down," he said, holding up her gloved fingers, and bowing over them. "You are my nearest neighbor, and yet you have never called upon me."

She followed him into his sitting-room, and took the easy chair he wheeled out toward the table for her. It was a larger apartment than the narrow staircase and cramped landing had promised. The ceiling was low and dreadfully smoky, it was true, and the appointments and furniture were old-fashioned. But the whole effect, if somewhat meager and unadorned, was comfortable and honest.

"Put off your hat and gloves, and look as if you felt at home," urged David. "You've but a step to go."

He busied himself meanwhile in bringing from a recess of the sideboard two tumblers, a heavy decanter filled with an amber liquid, and a big bottle of soda water.

"You'll join me in some whisky and soda?" he asked pleasantly, fumbling with the wire.

"Oh mercy, no!" said Vestalia. "Really I mustn't touch anything more. I see now that I have been drinking far too much, all day long."

"Tut!" he answered. "How could there be too much on a birthday? And now I think of it, there were two of them! I pledge my word, it has been a singularly dry occasion for a double birthday. We must hasten to make good the deficiency."

Vestalia had drawn off her gloves. She rose now, and standing before the mantel-mirror, lifted her hat from her head. Then she turned and, half-playfully, half in pleading, shook her bright curls at him. "I thought it was going to be different hereafter," she said, softly.

He looked inquiry for an instant, then nodded comprehension. "Ay," he said, with gravity, "you're a wise virgin. This one glass shall last me the night. You are very welcome here, my lady!"

She smiled at the lifted tumbler, over which his eyes regarded her. "What lots of books you have!" she exclaimed, a moment later, and began an inspection of the room, lingering in turn before each of the old prints on the dingy walls, and examining the rows of volumes in detail. He loitered beside her for a little, passing comments on what seemed to interest her. Then he disappeared in an adjoining room, and returned in a loose velveteen jacket and slippers. He took the famous dressing-bag from the table.

"Your visit isn't at all over yet," he remarked; "but I am consumed with a desire to see you sitting opposite me, here, in those wee soft slippers of yours. It will make a sweet picture for me to carry into dreamland. And so first I will show you your new home."

She followed him out into the hall, and then through the doors he unlocked into the apartments of the mysterious "Mr. Linkhaw." The first room disclosed itself, when the gas was lit, to be similar to David's in size, but all else was strangely different.

The Turkey red carpet was brilliant, almost garish, in its newness, and the ceiling was covered with a bright pink paper. All round three sides were broad divans, heaped with soft red cushions and downy pillows. No chairs were to be seen. More singular still, the walls were crowded with the stuffed heads of animals—bisons, bears, moose, elks, antelopes, wolves, and endless varieties of deer. Vestalia gazed at these trophies of the chase with surprise.

"Linkhaw is a mighty hunter before the Lord," Mosscrop explained. "Yon is the bedroom. It is fairly carpeted with the skins of tigers, lions, leopards, and such like beasts. If you dream of jungles and Noah's ark tonight, and don't like it, we'll throw them all out in the morning."

"But what am I doing in this Mr. Link-haw's rooms?" inquired the girl. "I don't understand it at all. Suppose he should come?"

David laughed lightly. "It's a far cry from Uganda to Dunstan's Inn. Or maybe he's in the Hudson Bay Territory. It's a year and more since I knew of his whereabouts. The most unheard-of and God-forgotten wilderness on earth—that's where you may always count on his being, unless he has learned of some still more impossible and repellent wild, just discovered, in the meantime. He is an old friend and school-fellow of mine, and leaves his keys with me. I just have a look at the place now and then, to keep the laundress up to the mark."

He passed on into the bedroom, struck a light, and threw a scrutinizing glance round. "You'll be needing fresh sheets and the like," he said, returning. "I'll bring them."

He came back with an armful of linen, and heaped it on the bed. "Now you're right as a trivet," he cried, cheerily. "Everything has been aired. And now I'll be waiting for you to come back to me, with the pretty little slippers. Mind, I'm capable of great excesses in drink if you delay over-long."

Vestalia's delay was inconsiderable. They sat for an hour or more, she with the dainty new footgear on the fender, he, lounging low in his chair, stretching out his own feet close to the rail beside hers.

"I could wish it were winter," he mused, once, "so that we might have a fire. We have an old saying about two pairs of slippers on the hearth. I never thought before what homely beauty there was in it. Ah, there'll be cool nights coming on now, and then we'll start a blaze. But even with a black grate, it is the dearest evening of my life."

"And of mine," responded the girl.

Hours later, David still sat by the empty fireplace, and ruminated over his pipe. He had put the decanter and glass resolutely back into the sideboard, and turned a key on them. He had taken down a book, but it lay unregarded on the floor beside him. He desired to do nothing but think, and yet even that it was not easy to contrive. Thoughts would not marshal themselves in any ordered sequence.

The whole day had yielded an extraordinary experience, involving all thoughts of momentous possibilities, which he said over and over again to himself demanded the coolest and most conservative consideration. But when he strove to fasten his mind to the task, straightway it swerved and curveted and danced off beyond control.

One memory returned to him ceaselessly: the way Vestalia had risen finally to say good-night, and insisted strenuously on his not quitting his chair, and then, all at once, had bent swiftly down and kissed him before she ran from the room. And well, why not? he asked himself at last; why shouldn't he abandon himself to remembering it? What else was there equally well worth recalling?

The early morning on the bridge rose again before him; the tenderly compassionate intimacy which, stealing slowly over them, seemed yet to have burst forth in ripe fullness from the very beginning; the delightful meals together, the long walks and talks, the little gifts which brought such happiness to the donor; the languorously saddened twilight on the river, the silent homecoming, the surprise, the kiss—so the sweet chain of reverie coiled and unfolded itself, with quickened heart-beats for links.

Once a thought came to him—a thought which seemed hard and cold as his native granite, and rough with the bristling spikes of his own hillside heather—that he had spent in that one day more than his whole week's income. In other times the fact would have disturbed David. Now he looked it calmly in the face, and smiled at it derisive dismissal. The savings of a year, or of four years—what were even they when weighed in the balance against the fact that next door, under these very roof-beams, the dear Vestalia was peacefully sleeping?

It must have been long after midnight when, in the act of filling his pipe once more, it occurred to him to go to bed instead. Upon reflection, he was both tired and sleepy.

He rose and yawned, and then smiled upon his own image in the mirror at remembering how happy he was as well. It was a queer mess, to be sure, but there was no element in it which he regretted or would have changed. It was all delicious, through and through.

As he glanced again at his reflection in the glass, and warmed his heart by the flame of triumphant joy which gleamed through the eyes he looked into, a sudden rhythmical noise rose upon the profound stillness of the old inn. It caught his ear, and he turned to listen.

"It is that blessed creature snoring—breathing, I mean," was his first thought. But no, it was in too rapid a measure for that. Then the sound waxed louder, and he recognized that it was of footsteps steadily ascending the stairs. "The watchman, coming to make sure of the lights," he thought, with re-assurance.

But this hypothesis fell to the ground also.

The footsteps mounted to the landing close outside. The noise ceased, and then there came the unmistakable jingle of a key— nay, the very grating of it in the lock of the door opposite.

David's veins, for a confused moment, ran cold. Then, with an excited ejaculation, he ran to his door, and flung it open.

"Stop that, you idiot!" he commanded, in muffled but ferocious tones.

"Ah, Davie, Davie! Still at the bottle!" replied a well-known voice from out of the obscurity.

Chapter 6

Mosscrop groaned at recognition of the voice in the dark.

"Of all inopportune creatures in the animal kingdom!" he bewailed under his breath. "Sh! for Heaven's sake, man, don't talk so loud. Come inside here, and walk softly."

"What is it you're stalking, Davie—snakes?" queried the newcomer, with obvious sarcasm. But he lowered his voice, and came forward into David's room. The latter closed the door noiselessly, and drew a long sigh of consolation. The two men looked at each other for a minute in silence.

"You don't mean that there are burglars in the house?" asked the intruder. A gleam of hopeful light shone in his eyes as he spoke, then died down at David's shake of the head.

The Earl of Drumpipes, in the peerage of Scotland, was a year younger than his friend the Culdee Professor. The gaslight revealed him now to be a tall, burly, rubicund man, with a broad, strongly-marked face of a severe aspect. His yellowish hair was cut close over a head which seemed unduly large for even his powerful frame, and was thinning towards baldness on the top. The collar of a woolen shirt showed a good deal of his thick neck, burnt a bright red at the back by a fiercer sun than warms these British islands. His prominent blue eyes bulged forth more than ever, now, in mystified inspection of David's countenance. While he still gazed, it occurred to him to hold out his hand, as mighty as a blacksmith's, in perfunctory greeting, and David took it with an effusiveness which was novel to them both.

"I'm really delighted to see you, Archie. I give you my word I am!" he protested, eagerly.

"You have your own way of showing it," growled the other. "Yet you seem sober enough. What ails you, man?"

"Oh, the strangest story!" said David. "Sit down here, and I'll get out the whisky." He busied himself between the sideboard and table, talking as he did so, while the other sprawled his large bulk in one of the easy chairs and lit a pipe.

"See here, Drumpipes, damn it all," he began, "I'm a gentleman, am I not?"

"You are a professional man, a person of education," the Earl assented, cautiously.

"Well, this is the first day in long years that I have felt like a gentleman."

"You were ever a bit susceptible to hallucinations, Davie," said the other. "There's a streak of unreality in your nature. Hold there! Not so much soda. I'm sore in need of a bath, I know; but everything at its proper time. Well, go on—how are you accounting for this extraordinary occurrence? You've felt all day like a gentleman! It arouses my curiosity."

"Chuck that, Archie, or you'll hear nothing at all."

"Very well, my boy. I'll just drink this, then, and go to my bed. It will be welcome, I can tell you."

He drained the tumbler, and made as if to rise. David hurled himself forward with a restraining arm. "Don't be an ass, old man! I've told you once, you mustn't go near your place tonight," he urged petulantly. "I'll give you my bed, and I'll sleep on the sofa here. It's all right, I assure you. If you must know, there is somebody sleeping in your room."

The Earl frowned up at his friend. "That was not in the bargain, Mosscrop," he said, with sharpness. "I don't like it."

"All I can say is," retorted David, "that if you'd been in my place you'd have done the same thing—or no, I'm not so sure about that; but under the circumstances it was the only thing I could do. It's a young lady who is occupying your room, Drumpipes."

"Aha!" cried the Earl, "let's have her out! I'm not so sleepy as I thought. You can do something in the way of a supper, can't you?"

"No, I can't, and if I could I wouldn't. You misapprehend the situation entirely, my friend. This is a poor girl who——" and David went on and told, in brief fashion, the story of the day.

"Nine pounds odd your whistle cost you, eh, Davie?" was the listener's comment, at the conclusion of the narrative. "Well, each man has his own notion of what he wants for his money. It is not mine, I'll say frankly. And what's the program for tomorrow? South Kensington Museum and Hampton Court? The next day you might do the Tower and Epping Forest. Then Westminster Abbey and Richmond—but you'll come soon to the end of your rope. And sooner, still, I'm thinking, to the end of your banking account."

"That's my affair," returned Mosscrop, testily.

"I might be said to have some small concern in the matter," Drumpipes observed, "seeing that I provide furnished lodgings for this beautiful experiment in combined philanthropy and instruction. But you're drinking nothing."

"No; I had my one glass before you came. I'm taking care of myself these days."

"And high time, too!" admitted the candid friend. "I'll not say you'll not be the better for it."

"Well, and don't you see?" urged Mosscrop, with earnestness, "it's just the fact of her being there yonder that makes it seem worth while to go to bed sober. It alters my whole conception of myself. It gives me entirely new ideas of what I ought to do. So long as I led this solitary life here there was nothing for me but to drink. But it's different now."

The Earl grinned. "And how long will you be content to have this improving influence radiated to you from across the passage?" he asked, with cynicism. "Supposing, of course, that I give up my rooms to the reform-dynamo, so to speak."

"Oh, of course, no one is asking that of you. Obviously, your return makes other arrangements imperative."

"What will the other arrangements be like?"

"That remains to be seen. But I'm quite clear about one thing. I will not turn back from what I have undertaken. She shall not know what want is, and she shall be respected. I swear that, Drumpipes; and I want you to remember it."

"Oh, I respect her immensely already," said the Earl. "By George, a girl must possess extraordinary qualities who can come out early and catch a Professor of Culdees off her own bat, and work him for a tenner, and then leave him to forswear whisky on one side of a passage while she sleeps the sleep of the just in borrowed apartments on the other. It's really splendid, old man. I take off my hat to her."

"Archie," remarked David, slowly, "I'm smaller than you are, and no athlete, God knows; but if we have any more of that I will hit you in the eye, and chance it."

Drumpipes was amused at the notion, and chuckled. Then his face and voice lapsed into solemnity. "Davie," he said, "I've no wish to vex you, but it's a bad business. You'll not win your way through without much expense and soreness of heart. You can take that from me, who should know if any man does."

Mosscrop accepted the portentous gravity of the tone in good faith. He nodded, as he looked hard at his friend.

"Ay, I know," he said, softly. "But I have no despair, and few doubts about it all, Archie. I am very happy in the thought of going forward with it; so happy that I see I never knew what happiness meant before. And if—we'll put it at the worst possible —if disappointment should come out of it, why, I shall already have had the joy. And even if it broke me, what would it matter? I should only be back again where I was yesterday, and no one on earth would be the worse for that. But with you it was different."

The Earl nodded in turn, and smoked his pipe. At last, without lifting his voice or disclosing special interest in his hews, he said, "Man, she's dead."

David's eyes dilated. "What's that—she—your wife, do you mean, is dead?"

"Ay, four months since," replied the other quietly.

Mosscrop came over and shook hands with his friend. "I will take a drink with you, after that," he said, and filled a glass. "Tell me about it."

"I know nothing about it—except that she is dead. That is enough, quite enough." He lifted his tumbler. "Here's to the heating arrangements in the warmest corner down below."

"A foul cat!" said David, with a harsh tremor in his voice, sipping the toast.

"A very pretty woman," answered the Earl, musingly. "Hair like a new primrose, face like an earl Christian martyr, dearest little feet you ever imagined. You never saw her. You would have wanted to die for her on the spot. She would have made a single bite of you, my friend. I was a good deal tougher mouthful, but I got mangled more or less in the operation. These are the things that make one grateful for the religious influences of childhood. I should be downhearted just now if I were not able to believe in a Hell."

"There is no doubt about the thing—she is really dead?"

"Dead as a mackerel, thank God. My lawyers certify to the blessed event. They ought to know. They have stood in the breach for four years, warding off writs, injunctions, mandamuses, and appeals, with which she and the unscrupulous scoundrels, her solicitors, bombarded them. The costs those ancient parties must have charged up against me! Man, I'm fair frightened to go into the City and face them. There are three attempts at judicial separation, one divorce suit, two petitions for restoration of conjugal rights, three examinations of witnesses by commission, four appeals—the thought of those bills sickens me, Davie."

"You're well out of the noose at any cost."

"Well, then, if your neck is free, keep it so, man!"

David smiled with gentle self-assurance.

"Ah, laddie, if you could have seen the innocence of her. She drank Capri at breakfast, and then champagne at luncheon, and more of the same at dinner, with old tawny port on top of it—all as trustingly and confidingly as a babe. It softened one's heart to see her lack of guile, her pretty inexperience."

The Earl sniffed audibly. "Oh, ay, it's a beautiful spectacle, no doubt, and very touching. The pity is that magistrates will not always view it in that light next morning. But then so many things look different in the morning."

Again Mosscrop smiled. "Save your moans, Archie," he advised, "till you see her yourself. You'll meet the lady at breakfast."

"I'm damned if I do," said Drumpipes.

"Now then, you're talking like an idiot. You, a hunter of lions and crocodiles and wild asses of the desert, to turn tail and run from one wee yellow-headed lassie! and desert an old friend, moreover, who needs your advice and judgment in the most important matter of his life! You know you're flatly incapable of it."

"I'll not promise to be civil to her if I stop," the other growled. "The mere thought of yellow-haired women is nauseating to me. Why on earth, man, if you must make a stark-staring lunatic of yourself, could you not hit on a decent and reputable color?"

"Never a dye has touched it," protested David. "It's as natural as the sunshine—and as radiant."

"Then you're a ruined man, Davie," the Earl gravely declared, between puffs at his pipe. "There may be some saving quality in a woman who merely dyes her hair. An honest nature may persist beneath the painted wig, in spite of her endeavors. But if she's a tortoise-shell tabby born, then you might better be dead than sitting there mooning about her. I give you up as a lost creature!"

"Then all the more reason you should help me to cook a fine breakfast, to confront my doom upon," replied Mosscrop, lightly. "I didn't quite promise that I'd call her in time to assist. It will be more of a surprise to have it all ready, spread in her honor, when she comes in. What do you think of soft roes grilled on toast, eh? You can get them in tins. And some little lamb cutlets—or perhaps venison—and then some eggs Bercy—you do those fit for a queen, and we might have——"

"The truth is," put in the other, reflectively, "that black is the only wholly satisfying hair for a woman. The intervening compromises—all the browns and chestnuts and reds and auburns—are a delusion. I see that very clearly now. Give me the hair that throws a purplish shadow, glossy and thick and growing well down upon the forehead, and then a straight-nosed face, wide between the eyes and rounded under the chin, and a complexion of a soft, pale olive. There's nothing else worth talking about."

"I had thought of those small Italian sausages, but I don't know that in hot weather they——"

"Oh rot!" said the nobleman. "Who wants to talk about muffins and ham fat at this time of night? Have you no poetry in you, man? There was a divine creature on the steamer coming over—great eyes like a sloe, and the face of a Circassian princess, calm, regal, languid, yet with depths of passion underneath that seemed to call out to you to risk your immortal soul for the sake of drowning in them——"

"My word, here is cheek, if you like!" burst in Mosscrop, stormily. "You won't let me talk about my girl at all; you sneer and gibe and croak evil suspicions, and make a general nuisance of yourself at the least mention of her—and then you suppose I'm going to sit patiently and listen to such blithering twaddle as this. Damn it all, a man's got some rights in his own room!"

"I'm told not," commented the Earl, grimly.

"Now, why hark back to that?" demanded David, with a show of petulance. "It's all settled and done with, hours ago. But what I was saying was, it isn't the decent thing for you to—to obtrude talk of that sort just to throw ridicule on a subject that I feel very keen about."

Drumpipes yawned frankly. "It's time you turned in, Davie," he remarked. "The lack of sleep aye makes you silly. I've no wish to ridicule your subject, as you call her. It's not at all necessary. You'll see for yourself how ridiculous it is in the morning. It merely occurred to me that if we must talk of women, I'd something in my mind worth the while—no strolling yellow-headed vagrant picked up at random on a bridge, but a gentlewoman in education and means and manners. Man, you should see her teeth when she smiles!"

"Archie," replied David, solemnly, "I should think your own better instincts might prompt you to recall that you've only been a widower four months."

"Four months?—Four hundred years!" cried the Earl, stoutly. He reached round and replenished his glass. "It is with the greatest difficulty that I recall any detail of the matrimonial state. Already the memory of my first pair of breeks is infinitely fresher to me than any of it. In another week or so the last vestige of a recollection of it will be clean gone. And a good riddance, too!"

"It was an ill thought to remind you of it," admitted Mosscrop. "Devil take all women—or all but one——"

"And she black-haired," interposed the Earl.

"Deuce seize them all but two, then, for the rest of the night. Where have you been the long year-and-a-half, Archie?"

"Just looking about me," replied the other, with nonchalance. "Bechuanaland for a time, but it's sore overrated. Then I had a shy at the Gaboon country, but there's a conspiracy among the niggers to protect the gorilla—I think he's a sort of uncle of theirs —and a white man can do no good by himself. I thought there might be some decent sport over in Brazil, where they advertised a revolution on, and I tried to travel around with the rebels for a while, but it wasn't up to much. You brought down an occasional half-breed Portugueser with epaulettes on, but you couldn't eat them, and you didn't want them stuffed at any price; and besides, when you came to find out, the whole war was merely a fight between two firms of coffee-traders in New York, and that wasn't good enough. I tell you what, though," he went on, with more animation, "Arizona is damned good fun. I haven't seen anything better anywhere than a good, square cattle-lifter hunt. They got up three or four, just on my account, I imagine, after they found I could ride, and shoot at a gallop. The charm of the thing is that there's no close season for cattle-thieves, and they're game to the death, I tell you. I got potted twice, and once they let daylight straight through me. I had to lie up for repairs for nearly three weeks. They went and hung the fellow while I was in bed. We had words about that. I insisted it wasn't sportsmanlike—and that they ought to have given him a horse, and then sprung him out of a trap or something of that sort, and let him have a run for his money, the same as we do with rabbits that the ferrets bring up. But they couldn't see it, and so I turned it up and came North. They'll ruin the whole thing, though, if they don't chuck that foolish hanging business. The first thing they know, everybody'll stop running off cattle, just as a protest, and then their place won't be worth living in. It'll be a pity, because a cowboy gone wrong is really the best thing there is. He's as good as a Bengal tiger and a Russian wolf together, with a grizzly bear thrown in. You may quote me as saying so."

"I shall not fail to do so," said David. "Come, drink up your liquor, and we'll toddle. I'm fair glad to see you back whole and sound, laddie—and more still, a free man."

He brought forth from the bedroom a pillow and some blankets, and began arranging them upon the sofa. "And are the Americans so daft about lords and titles as they're made out?" he asked as he worked. "Did they humble themselves before the handle to your name?"

Drumpipes sat up. "Do you suppose I'm such an abandoned ass as to travel with a title?" he demanded. "Man, if you knew what it cost me, even without it, it would turn your hair grey. Ten dollars here, twenty dollars there, seven dollars and a-half somewhere else—one steady and endless drain on the purse, till the marvel is I was able to get out at all! And there's no third-class on the railways whatever. It's just terrible, Davie! And as ill-luck would have it, I couldn't even come home steerage on the steamer. There were passengers that I knew in the first cabin, and so I had to throw away more money there. And I'm not like you—I've no ten-pound notes to spare for my day's amusement."

"No, you're not like me," responded Mosscrop, in no sympathetic tone. "I have my magnificent £432 per annum, which is over eight guineas a week. And you—you have only a paltry four thousand odd, not more than ten times as much. I wonder you've kept off the rates so long, Archie."

"Ah, I know all that," protested the Earl. "But you have no damned position to keep up. You must remember that, Davie, It's a very important fact. It makes all the difference in the world."

"But you only keep it up in your own mind, and that's not an expensive place. There's been no year since I first knew you, either as Master of Linkhaw or since you came into the whole of it, that you've spent the half of your income. To hear you talk, one would think you'd been scattering your capital as well with both hands."

"Ah, but those lawyers' bills, Davie! What think you now should they be like? Six hundred, eh? Or may be seven?"

"You'll know soon enough. I'll not encourage you to pass a sleepless night. Come now. You've got things in your bag here, haven't you? I can let you have whatever you lack."

"No, you keep your bed. I'll sleep out here," said Drumpipes. "I'm a deal more used to roughing it than you are. I give you my word, I shall sleep here like a top."

Mosscrop strove to resist, but his friend was resolute, and the sofa had to be surrendered to him. He rose, yawning, and began to throw off his outer garments. "I've paid as high as eleven shillings for a bedroom for one night in New York city!" he affirmed, drowsily, "although, to give the Devil his due, they make no charge for candles and soap. Man, if they'd known I was an Earl, they'd have lifted all seven of my skins."

"Oh, but they have a reputation for acumen," urged Mosscrop, drily. "They'd have comprehended fine that you were but a Scotch Earl. Good night!"

The broad daylight woke David up nearly an hour later than it should have done. He had produced upon himself during the night an impression of sleeping very little—and that a light and dainty slumber, ready and eager on the instant of need to dissolve into utter wakefulness. Yet it was the fact, none the less, that he had ingloriously overslept himself. The watch on his table pointed to half-past eight.

He hurriedly drew on some of his garments, and stepped into the sitting-room to rouse the Earl. To his great surprise that nobleman had disappeared. The tumbled bed-clothes showed where he had slept. There was his hand-bag, duly packed and closed, at the foot of the sofa.

Reasoning that Drumpipes had not promised to breakfast, and was a perverse creature anyway, and probably had been worried by early brooding over those lawyers' bills into a restless mood, Mosscrop returned to his room, and completed the work of dressing. He shaved with exceptional care, and bestowed thought upon the selection of a neck-tie. It occurred to him that he had some better clothes than those he had worn yesterday, and, though he begrudged the time, the temptation to make the change was irresistible. He did not regret yielding, when he surveyed his full-length image in the mirror on his wardrobe door. He seemed to himself to look years younger than he had done before that momentous birthday. He smiled and nodded knowingly at the happy and confident face in the glass.

Under the circumstances, he should need help with the breakfast. The midnight notion of getting everything ready before he called his guest, submitted to abandonment without a murmur. He reverted joyfully to the original idea of letting her share all the delightful fun of preparing the meal. His fancy played with sportive tenderness about the picture of her, here in his tiny scullery which served as a kitchen, her sleeves rolled up, a towel pinned round her waist for an apron, actually cooking things for them both to eat. Very likely he knew more about that sort of thing than she did; he beheld himself giving her instructions, as they bent together over the big gas cooking-stove. Could anything be more deliciously homelike than that?

That contrary, cross-grained Drumpipes had predicted that the whole thing would seem ridiculous to him in the morning. He affirmed to himself with fervor that it seemed more charming than ever as he went out into the passage, and knocked on the opposite door.

There seemed to be no answering sound, and he struck the panel more sharply, with his ear lowered to the keyhole. Still no response came.

"I am going to Covent Garden for a few minutes," he called through the keyhole; "shall I find you ready to help me when I get back?"

Since this, too, brought no reply, he took out his duplicate key and cautiously opened the door. The question, repeated in a much louder tone, died away in profound silence. The glass eyes of a moose on the wall opposite stared at him with an uncomfortable fixity.

The bedroom door was ajar, and David was emboldened to stride forward and beat smartly on it with his fist. Again he did this, and then, while a strange excitement welled upward within him—or was it a sinking movement instead?—flung the door open and looked in.

There was no Vestalia here at all!

The details that the bed was neatly made up, that the room showed no trace of recent occupancy, and that the dressing-bag was gone, soaked themselves vaguely through his mind. He looked about, both in this and the outer apartment, for a message of some kind, quite in vain.

His pained attention wandered again in haphazard fashion to the head of the moose, fastened between two windows. The fatuous emptiness of its point-blank gaze suddenly infuriated him, and he dealt its foolishly elongated snout a resounding whack with his open hand. The huge trophy toppled under the blow, swung half-loose on its fastening, then pitched with a crash to the floor.

Mosscrop kicked it violently again and again where it lay.

Chapter 7

Mosscrop had not the heart to breakfast alone in his deserted lodgings.

The impulse to get away mastered him on the instant of its appearance. He strode forth as if delay were fraught with sore perils. At a shabby luncheon-bar in the Strand below he consumed a cup of abominable coffee and a dry sausage-roll in the same nervous haste. The barmaid in attendance was known to him. She annoyed him now by displaying in her manner the assumption that he wished to laugh and joke with her as usual. He glowered at her instead, and met her advances to conversation with a curt nod.

"You must have got out of the wrong side of the bed this morning," she commented loftily.

"Very likely," he answered with cold brevity, counting out the necessary coppers and turning on his heel.

Outside he seemed to himself to choose the direction of his steps quite at random. He walked slowly, trying to fasten his brain down to the task of conjecturing what on earth it all meant. Alas, his mind was as empty as those desolate rooms up at the top of Dunstan's Inn. The power of coherent speculation had left him. It was hardly possible even to arrange in decent sequence the details of what had happened. An indefinitely sweeping rage at destiny in general oppressed all his faculties. He muttered meaningless oaths under his breath as he went along, directed at an intangible "it" which was equally without form and personality, a mere abstract symbol of the universal beastliness of things.

The notion of cursing Vestalia did not suggest itself. So far as he had any intelligible thoughts about her, they were instinctively exculpatory. She seemed indeed to have behaved stupidly, but it must have been under a misapprehension of some sort. Something perverse had happened to lead her off into a foolish course of action. He resolutely declined to open his mind to any other view of her. She must have quitted the Inn for some reason which wholly satisfied her sense of honorable conduct. What was this reason? Had she conjured it up out of her own meditations, or had it been furnished to her from an external source?

All at once he stopped short, mental and bodily progress alike arrested by a striking thought. "Damn him!" he murmured to himself, as he turned this new idea over. How that it had come to him, he fairly marveled at the dullness which had failed to discover it at the beginning. It was as plain as the nose on one's face—the Earl had bidden Vestalia to begone. "Ah, that miserly, meddling fool of a Drumpipes!" he groaned, between clenched teeth.

This laying bare of the mystery brought no consolation. The day was as irretrievably ruined, the tender little romance as ruthlessly crushed, as ever. A certain doubtful solace seemed to offer itself in the shape of a quarrel with Drumpipes, but Mosscrop shook his head despondently at it. What good would that do? And for that matter, how should one go to work to quarrel with that tough-hided, fatuous, conceited, dense-witted, imperturbable, and impenetrable idiot? He would never even perceive that the attempt was being made. David piled up in reverie the loathly epithets upon the over-large bald head of his friend with a savage satisfaction. "You preposterous clown!" he snarled at the burly blond image of the absent nobleman in his mind's eye. "You gratuitous and wanton ass! Oh, you unthinkable duffer!"

And somehow there was after all a kind of relief in these comminatory exercises. The dim light of a possible diversion began to filter through the storm-cloud of Mosscrop's wrath. He was still bitterly depressed, and furious as well, of course, but self-possession was returning to him, and with it the capacity for planning and ordering his movements. It occurred to him that he ought to do something to turn his thoughts temporarily at least from this world-weary sadness.

Up on the opposite corner his eye caught the legend "Savoy Street." He stared at the small sign, perched above the dingy brick cornice of the first-floor, for a moment with an unreflecting gaze. Then he turned and walked briskly down the steep hillside thoroughfare, and into the courtyard of the great hotel which, like the street and the quarter, commemorates in its name the first of a long and steadfast line of needy Continental princes whose maintenance the British tax-payer has found himself fated to provide.

At the desk, he wrote out a card and sent it up as an accompaniment to the inquiry whether Mr. Laban Skinner was in or not.

No, it was reported; Mr. Skinner had gone out—but the young lady was in.

David pondered this unexpected intelligence. "Did she tell you that she was in?" he asked the boy, suspiciously.

Yes; she had done so.

Mosscrop discovered that he had been quite unprepared for this. He knit his brows and ruminated upon it. His impression had been at the time that the girl disliked him, or at least disliked the proposition which her absurd father had made. It seemed to him, moreover, that he disliked, her in turn. She had stared rudely at poor Vestalia—but then it should be remembered in fairness that all women did that to one another. Her attitude towards him had been ostentatiously apathetic, almost to the point of insolence; and yet he recalled that in that moment when he had caught her unawares, she had been displaying a notable interest in what was going on. The notion that there had been a sort of challenge underlying the mask of studied indifference she had presented to him returned to his mind. And he still needed diversion, too, as much as ever.

"If you will show the way," he said to the boy at this juncture.

The lift bore them a long distance upward, quite to the roof it seemed. David formed the impression that rents must be cheap at that altitude; but when he took the first glance round the sitting-room into which he found himself ushered, the idea vanished.

It was a large and imposingly-appointed room, exhaling, as it were, an effect of high-priced luxury. The broad windows at the front came down to the floor, and opened upon a balcony. There were awnings hung outside to ward off the sunshine, and this threw the whole apartment into a mellow twilight, contrasting sharply with the brightness of the corridor Mosscrop had just quitted.

He looked about him, hesitatingly, to make sure that there really was no one in the room. The glimpse of some white drapery fluttering against the edge of a chair out on the balcony caught his eye, and he moved across to the nearest open window.

The noble prospect of the Thames viewed from this height impressed itself with great vividness upon his mind, even in advance of his perception that he had indeed found Miss Skinner. He looked downward with a gaze which embraced both the girl and the river, and for a moment they preserved an equally unconscious aspect.

The young lady then lifted her head, sidewise, and acknowledged Mosscrop's presence by a slow drooping movement of her black lashes. "How do you do?" she remarked, placidly. "Bring out a chair for yourself."

He did as he was told, and seated himself near the balustrade, so that he partially faced her; but he looked again at the wonderful picture below, to collect his thoughts.

"I had no idea it was so magnificent up here," he said at last.

"Indeed," commented his companion. It was impossible to say whether the remark was in the nature of an exclamation or an inquiry. Mosscrop found himself compelled to glance up, if only to determine this open question.

The realization that she was extremely well worth looking at swept over him like a flood, at the instant of his lifting his eyes. It suited her to be bare-headed, and to wear just the creamy white cashmere house-gown that he beheld her in. The glossy plaits and masses of her hair were wonderful. In the softened, tinted half-shadow of the awning her dark skin glowed with a dusky radiance which fascinated him. Her mien was as imperious as ever, but it suggested now an empress disposed to play, a sultana whose inclination was for amusement.

"Did you come up to see the view? I daresay it is even better from the leads. You call them leads here, don't you? Your novels always do, I know."

This speech of hers, languidly delivered, had its impertinent side, without doubt, but Mosscrop caught in its tone a not unamiable intention. She did not smile in response to the puzzled questioning of his swift glance, but he convinced himself none the less that it was a pleasantry. He noted in this instant of confused speculation that she had a book in her lap—a large, red-covered volume with much gilt on the binding—and that she kept a finger in it to mark some particular place.

"Your father was good enough to ask me to call," he reminded her, with gentleness.

"I asked for him, and I——" "You are disappointed to find him out?" Yes; there could be no doubt she was amusing herself.

"Oh, that depends," ventured David, with temerity.

The girl surveyed him at her leisure. "If I remember aright," she said, "you were invited conditionally. You were to come, or rather to communicate with us, if you decided to close with my father's offer. So I suppose you've made up your mind to accept."

"Well, I should like to talk more about it; get a clearer idea of what was proposed."

"My father takes great pains in expressing himself. I should have said his explanation was as full as anything could well be on this earth."

"To speak frankly," replied David, "I got the idea that you didn't care much about your father's scheme—in fact, that you disliked it. That's what I wanted to be clear about. It would be ridiculous for me to be going round, delivering instructive lectures to you on antiquities and ruins and so forth, and you hating me all the while for a bore and a nuisance. It would place us both in a false position."

"And you can't stand false positions, eh?"

Mosscrop rose. "I'm afraid I can't stand this one, at all events," he answered, with dignified brevity.

"Oh, you mustn't think of going!" his hostess protested, with a momentary ring of animation in her voice. "My father's liable to return any minute, and he'd be greatly put out to find he'd missed you."

"I could wait for him in the reception room downstairs," he suggested, moodily—"or, for that matter, I don't know that it's very important that we should meet at all."

"I don't call that a bit polite," she commented.

"I'm afraid your standards of politeness are beyond me," he began, formally. Then the absurdity of the thing struck him, and he grinned in a reluctant fashion. "Do you really want me to stay?" he asked, with the spirit of banter in his tone.

"Oh that depends," she mocked back at him. "If you can be amusing, yes."

"Just how amusing must I be?" He propped into his chair again, and this time laid his hat aside.

"Oh, say as much so as you were yesterday with the young lady of the butter-colored hair. I think that would about fill the bill."

Mosscrop ground his teeth with swift annoyance. Then he chuckled in a mood of saturnine mirth. Finally he sighed, and dolefully shook his head.

"Ah, yesterday!" he mourned, drawing a still deeper breath.

"You were extremely entertaining, then," pursued the other, ignoring his emotions. "Do you find yourself—as a usual thing, I mean—varying a good deal from day to day? I ask entirely from curiosity. I've never met anyone before in precisely your position."

"No, I should think not!" he assented, with gloomy emphasis. "I can well believe that my position is unique in the history of mankind. Such grotesque luck could scarcely repeat itself. But I beg your pardon—it isn't a thing that would interest you; I had no business to mention it at all."

"It was I who mentioned it, I believe," she corrected him calmly.

There was obvious meaning in her insistence. He looked up at her in vague surprise, the while he mentally retraced the steps by which the conversation had reached this point. There was undoubtedly a very knowing expression in her eyes. Clearly she had meant to associate Vestalia with what she described as his position—the position which she deemed so unusual; it was equally plain that she desired him to understand that she did so.

It was impossible that she should know anything of what had happened. He searched his memory, and made sure that no personal hint of any sort had drifted into that rambling discourse of his in the Assyrian corridors, which the Americans had more or less overheard. What then was she talking about?

Ah, what indeed? She lay back in her chair, and met his gaze of bewildered interrogation with a fine show of composure. She looked at him tranquilly through lazy, half-closed eyelids. His suspicions discerned beneath the passive surface of this regard animated under-currents of ironical amusement and triumph.

There was nothing overt upon which he could found the challenge to an explanation, but as he continued to scrutinize her, he could fancy that her whole presence radiated the suggestion of repressed glee. Whatever the mystery might be, she was extracting great delight from her possession of a clue to it.

"Yes, it was you who mentioned my position," he remarked, groping lamely for some sure footing on which to redress his disadvantage. "I don't know that! quite follow you; wherein do you find my position, as you term it, so exceptional?

"You yourself have boasted that it couldn't be matched in all history," she reminded him. Her tone was casual enough, but the sense of sport began to gleam unmistakably in her eyes.

"Now you argue in a circle," he remonstrated, with a shade of professional acerbity in his voice. "Your remark came before mine, and hence cannot possibly have been based upon my subsequent comment. If I may be permitted the observation, they seem to teach logic but indifferently in the United States."

"Oh, that is why we came here," retorted the girl, with ostentatious naïveté. The conceit pleased her so much that she bent forward, and assumed the manner of one communicating an important fact. "That is why I had my father make you an offer at once. You know, most professors, and teachers, and so on, are so hard to understand. But the moment I laid eyes on you I said, 'There's a man that I can see through as if he were plate-glass; I can read him like a book.' And, of course, that must be the most valuable of all qualities in an instructor."

"So I am entirely transparent, am I? I present no secrets to your gaze?" Mosscrop spoke like one in whom pique and a sense of the comical struggled for mastery. "Then I cannot do better than beg you to tell me some things about myself. Why, for example, do I sit here patiently and submit to be laughed at, heckled, satirized, and generally bully-ragged by a young lady, whose title to do these things is not in the least apparent to me?"

"Why, don't you remember? You're waiting for papa."

"And incidentally providing his offspring, in the interim, with much harmless and chaste entertainment," put in Mosscrop, drily. "I am charmed to have diverted you so successfully. It occurs to me, since you are so readily amused, that you must have been awfully bored before I made my happy appearance."

"Oh, quite the contrary," exclaimed the girl, with a sudden stress in her tone, which hinted that this was what she had been waiting for. She opened the volume, as she spoke, at the place marked by her finger. "I was reading in the Peerage, you know. It is a most entrancing book. I am never dull when I am reading about earls and things."

"I have heard that the work enjoys a remarkable popularity in your country," David remarked, sourly.

"There is such romance in it!" she went on, in mock rhapsody; "it makes such appeals to the imagination! It puts you at once in an atmosphere of chivalry, of knightly adventures and exploits, of tournaments and chain-armor, and courts of love——"

"And of divorce, and bankruptcy, too," he interposed. "Don't forget those."

The girl looked grave for a moment, and nodded her head as if in relenting apology. Then she recovered her high spirits by as swift a transition.

"And such splendid old names as you get, too!" she continued, with her eyes on the open page. "Listen to this, for example. Could anything be finer?"

DRUMPIPES, Earl of. (Sir Archibald-Coro-nach-Dugal-Strathspey-Malcolm-Linkhaw) Viscount Dunfugle of Inverdummie, and Baron Pilliewillie of Slug-Angus, Morayshire, all in the peerage of Scotland, and a Baronet of Nova Scotia. Born August 24th, 1866. Succeeded his grandfather as 19th Earl January 10th, 1888. Married May 2nd, 1890, Janet-Eustasia-Marjory, 3rd daughter of the Master of Craigie-whaup by his wife, the Hon. Tryphena Pincock (who deceased March 6th, 1879), elder daughter of the 4th Baron Dubb of Kilwhissel. Seat, Skirl Castle, near Lossiewink, Elgin. Club, Wanderers.

She read it all with marked deliberation and distinctness of utterance. When she finished, silence reigned for some time on the balcony.

"Well, am I not right?" she asked at last, lifting her head, and flashing the full richness of her black eyes into Mosscrop's face. "Don't you admit the inspiration of such names?"

David answered in a hesitating, dubious manner. "I am more curious about the source—and scope—of your inspiration," he said. "Unhappily, it cannot be pretended that you are transparent. You confront me with an opacity against which my feeble wits beat in vain. I can see that it is known to you that I know Drumpipes. But why this fact should assume in your mind such portentous and mysterious dimensions, and why you should treat it with the air of one who has unearthed a great conspiracy, a terrible secret, I can't for the life of me comprehend."

"Ah, you are more complicated than I had thought," she replied. "I did not imagine you would keep up the defense so long."

"Me?—a defense? never," cried David, incited in some vague way by this remark to an accession of assurance. "I defend nothing. I surrender with eagerness. I roll myself at your feet, Miss Skinner. All I crave in return is that you will put a label on my submission. It may be weak, but I should dearly like to know what it is that I am abandoning."

"What I should suggest that you give up is your attempt to deceive me—us—as to your identity."

"Ah! am I indeed someone else, then? Upon my word, I can't congratulate the other fellow."

"You wrote your name down for my father yesterday, and again on this card here this morning, as Mosscrop — David Mosscrop."

He assented by a nod, and allowed the beginnings of an abashed and contrite look to gather upon his face.

"Well, it just happened that, the moment I first laid eyes on you, I knew who you really were. By the merest accident, your picture had been shown to me—by a gentleman who knows you intimately, and is indeed distantly related to you—on shipboard coming over. I recognized you instantly, there in the Museum, and I made papa speak to you. I was curious to see what you would say and do."

"I'm afraid you were disappointed. Did you think I would shout and dance, or what?" He struggled with some degree of success to speak impassively.

"I had never met any one before in your position in life, and I had the whim to experiment on my own account." She said this as if defending her action to herself more than to her auditor.

"And may I have my little whim gratified too?" he asked. "I am extremely curious to know how you like your experiment as far as you have got with it."

She did not answer immediately, and he occupied the interval by an earnest mental scuffle after some clue to what she was driving at. He knew of no man who possessed his portrait—at least among those who went down to the sea in ships. He had had no photograph taken for years, to begin with. A distant relation of his, she had said, and on a very recent voyage from America. Who the deuce could it be? What acquaintance of his had been of late in America? All at once the answer leaped upward in his mind. He laughed aloud, with an abruptness which took him not less than his companion by surprise. But then a puzzled scowl overshadowed the grin on his countenance. He saw a little way farther into the millstone, but that was all.

"I hope you don't regret your experiment," he repeated. "It would have been simpler, perhaps, if your father had mentioned that you were friends of Mr. Linkhaw's. That in itself would have been an ample introduction."

"Perhaps we should have done so, had you been alone." Her tone was cool to the verge of haughtiness.

He rapidly considered what this might mean. Her remark clearly indicated that Vestalia's presence had seemed to her reprehensible. Why? There was some intricacy here which he could not fathom. That confounded Drumpipes had told her— what?

Eureka! He had it! The picture that she had seen was a little cheap ambrotype of Drumpipes and himself, standing together, which had been made by a poor devil of a wayside photographer, two Derby days before. Undoubtedly that was what the Earl had shown her—the only one he could have shown her. And—why of course—Drumpipes had pointed him, David, out as the Earl. What his motive could have been, heaven only knew, but this was palpably the key to the riddle.

He grasped this key with decision, on the instant. He straightened himself, frowned a little, and laboriously stiffened the tell-tale muscles about his mouth.

"I don't think I quite like this notion of Linkhaw's babbling about me and my affairs," he said, with austerity.

"Oh, I assure you," she protested, anxiously, "he was very cautious. He only gave the most sparing answers to my questions. I had to literally drag things from him."

"But what business had he showing my picture about to begin with? He shall hear what I think of it! Men's allowances have been stopped for less than that."

"It will be very unjust indeed if you visit it upon him," the girl urged, almost tremulously; "it was all my fault. I asked him one day if he had ever met a nobleman, and he, quite as a matter of course, mentioned that one of his own relatives was an Earl. One day, later, he was showing me a little tin-type of himself, and he merely said that you were the other person in the picture, that was all."

"And then you proceeded to drag things from him. I believe that was your phrase," remarked David, in a severe tone. The sensation of having this proud and insolent beauty in a tremor of entreaty before him was very delightful.

"Naturally, I asked him questions," she replied, with a little more spirit. "Earls don't grow on every bush with us. And for that matter, why, goodness me! he did nothing but praise you from morning till night. By his account, one would think butter wouldn't melt in your mouth. He made you out a regular saint. I was quite prepared to see you with a halo round your head—and instead, I——"

She stopped short, with a confused and deprecatory smile. David, noting it, rejoiced that he had taken a peremptory tone about the garrulous Linkhaw.

"Instead, you discovered that I was a mere flesh and blood mortal like the rest." He permitted himself to unbend, and even to smile a little, as he furnished this conclusion to her sentence. "Was it a very painful disillusionment?"

"Oh, I've read and heard enough about the lives that your class lead here in Europe," she replied, with a marked reversion toward her former manner. "I don't pretend that I was really surprised."

David assumed a judicial expression. "Considering the way we are brought up, and the temptations that are thrust upon us," he said, impartially, "I would not say that we are so much worse than other men."

"But you are pretty bad—that you must admit."

Before David had satisfactorily framed the admission expected of him, the sound of an opening door and of footsteps came from within.

"It is papa," whispered the girl, leaning forward in a confidential manner. "I'm going to tell him."

"I see no valid objection," answered David, with dignity.

Chapter 8

As the balcony was too small for another chair, and Mr. Skinner did not come to the window, his daughter led her guest into the sitting-room.

"Papa," she said, "you will recall the gentleman whom we met yesterday at the British Museum."

Mr. Skinner lifted to its place the pince-nez which depended on a gold thread from the lapel of his carefully-buttoned frock-coat, and scrutinized the person indicated in a painstaking manner.

"Ah, yes, indeed," he said, continuing his gaze, but with no salutation, and no offer of the hand.

"It's so dark in here, I don't believe you do," she remarked, to cover the awkwardness of the moment. "The sun has gone now, any way," and she moved back and put a hand upon the awning-cord.

"Permit me," said David, hurrying to her side, and pulling at the shade.

"He's out of sorts about something," the girl murmured furtively. "Don't mind it; just leave him to me."

In the brightened light, Mr. Skinner's demeanor seemed no more cordial. He regarded his visitor with a doubtful glance, and gave indications of a sense of embarrassment in his presence. The daughter, however, was in no respect dismayed by her responsibility.

"Papa," she said with brisk decision, "it was all a joke yesterday. Our friend was so amused by your offer yesterday——"

"I beg your pardon, Adele," the father interposed ceremoniously, "but it becomes immediately incumbent upon me to express my dissent. To obviate any possible misconception, it should be explicitly stated that, although it is true that the task of formulating the proposal to which you allude did undoubtedly devolve upon me, the proposition itself, both in spirit and suggestion, originated in your own consciousness."

"All right," she hurriedly went on, "have it anyway you like. The point is that this gentleman thought it was funny, and so he capped it with his own little joke by pretending to be some one else. He made up that name he gave you on the spur of the moment, just for sport. He came here this morning, just to explain. He was nervous about the deception, innocent though it was. Papa, let me introduce to you Mr. Linkhaw's relation, of whom he spoke so often, you know—the Earl of Drumpipes."

Mr. Skinner took in this intelligence with respectful deliberation. He bowed meanwhile, and, after a moment's deferential hesitation, shook hands in a formal way with David, and motioned him to a seat.

"Sir," he began, picking his phrases with even greater care, "you will excuse me if I do not address you as 'My Lord,' since it is a form of words which I cannot bring myself to regard as seemly when employed by one human being toward another; but I gather from my daughter's explanation that your statements yesterday concerning your identity were conceived in a spirit of pleasantry. Under ordinary circumstances, sir, the revelation that an entirely serious and decorous suggestion of mine had been received with hilarity might not convey to my mind an exclusively flattering impression. But I do not, sir, close my eyes to the fact that a wide gulf of usage and custom, and, I might say, of principles, separates a simple Jeffersonian Democrat like myself from the professor of an hereditary European dignity. I am therefore able, sir, to accept, with comparatively few reservations, the explanation which you have tendered to my daughter, and vicariously, as I understand it, to me."

David repressed a groan, and hastily cast about in his mind for a decent pretext for flight. "I assure you that it greatly relieves me to find you so courteously magnanimous," he said. "I merely yielded to the playful impulse of the moment; and as your daughter has so kindly told you, I made haste thereafter to repair my error, when its possible misinterpretation occurred to me." He bowed again, in response to the other's solemn genuflection, and looked toward the door.

"I should be pleased, sir," Mr. Skinner said, "if you would honor us by remaining to luncheon."

"Ah, I should have liked that so much," answered David, with fervor, "but unhappily I have an engagement at Marlborough House. It will be no end of a bore, but it can't be helped. An invitation there, you know, is equivalent to a command. That is one of the drawbacks of a monarchy—but of course every system has its weak points."

"That is a generalization," returned Mr. Skinner, "to which I am not prepared to give unmeasured adhesion. I will explain to you, sir, briefly, the reasons which dictate my hesitation to entirely——"

"I'm afraid, Mr. Skinner, that I must tear myself away," put in David, anxiously consulting his watch. "The Prince never forgives a fellow being late. He has to live so much on a timetable himself, you know, forever catching trains, and changing his uniforms, and turning up at the exact minute all over the place, laying cornerstones, and opening docks and unveiling statues, and so on, that it makes him intolerant of other people's lapses. And he's got a fearful memory for that sort of thing."

"I assume that you speak of the Heir Apparent," commented the other. "Am I to understand that you live in a state of personal subjection—that a nobleman in your position, for example, contemplates with apprehension the contingency of causing even the most trivial and transitory displeasure to the personage alluded to?"

"Apprehension, my dear sir? Positive horror! Ah, you little know the reality! Thoughtless people see us from the outside, and they lightly imagine that our lives are one ceaseless round of luxurious gaiety and gilded pleasure. They fancy that to have titles, to bear hereditary distinctions, to fill high places at Court, must be the sum of human happiness. Of course, I suppose we do have a better time than the average, but we pay a price for it. We smile, it is true, but there is always a shudder beneath the smile. A mere breath, a suspicion, the veriest paltry whim of royal disfavor, and we might better never have been born! And so," he finished with an uneasy graciousness, "you will understand my abrupt leave-taking now."

"I promise myself on another occasion, sir," said Mr. Skinner, with more warmth, "the privilege of discussing these topics with you at length. I do not deny that I am myself, today, somewhat preoccupied, and lacking in the power of intellectual concentration. Another occasion, I trust, will find me better fitted to bestow upon these subjects the alertness of comprehension and clarity of judgment which their importance demands. At the moment, I confess my mind is burdened with another matter."

"O, papa—you haven't gone and lost your letter of credit!" The girl intervened with accents of alarm.

The old gentleman shook his head, and smiled. "No," he replied, hesitatingly, "it is merely that I—I have been enjoined to secrecy about a very curious and interesting revelation which has been made to me, and concealment is profoundly alien to my nature. The necessity for maintaining a mysterious reserve weighs upon me, sir, with unaccustomed oppression."

"It is something that you have learned this morning?" demanded the daughter. "I'll make you tell me as soon as we're alone."

"Ah, that cannot be," the father answered. "My faith has been honorably pledged, and must be scrupulously observed."

"But surely it couldn't have been stipulated that I was not to know," she urged. "That would be absurd. And besides, who knows of even my existence over here?"

"Incomprehensible as it may appear to your perceptions," responded Mr. Skinner, "it happens that you were particularly alluded to in the terms of the confidential compact imposed upon me."

"Then you had no business to enter into it at all," she replied, vigorously. "Papa, I am surprised at you!"

There was something in his thoughts which lit the old gentleman's dry countenance with a transient gleam of enjoyment. "I hazard the humble opinion that your surprise will be appreciably augmented when, at the proper time, the truth shall have been revealed to you." He turned, with the flickerings of a whimsical smile in his eye, to their guest. "It is an extraordinary coincidence, sir; but you are also in a manner associated with the occult event to which I may not at present more pointedly refer."

David musingly looked the old gentleman in the eye. "Yes, I know," he answered; "but I agree with you that it should not be divulged to your daughter. As you have said, we men of the world are in duty bound to keep a decent veil drawn over certain phases of life. I am quite with you in that, sir; we cannot sufficiently respect and guard the sweet-minded innocence of our young ladies."

Mr. Skinner looked hard at the nobleman, and drew up his slender figure. "My memory, sir," he announced stiffly, "fails to recall any observation resembling in the slightest degree, either in form or sentiments, that which you have ascribed to me. Forgive me, sir, if I venture to further remind you that I have no desire to regard myself, or to be regarded, as a man of the world, in the sense in which I understand that term to be used by the aristocratic class in Great Britain."

The young lady seemed to share her father's feelings in the matter. "You must remember, Lord Drumpipes," she put in, coldly, "that our standards in such things are not yours. I daresay it seems natural enough to one in your position, and with your antecedents and associations, that a venerable, white-haired old gentleman should have disgraceful secrets which he ought to conceal from his family; but we take a different view of the meaning of the word 'gentleman,' and of the obligations which it involves."

"Ah, now I have offended you!" cried David, with a show of remorse. "I assure you that my only thought was to help your good father out of a fix. If I have done wrong, I beg you will put it down to my over-eagerness to be of assistance. And now," he stole a dismayed glance at his watch, "now I really must run. Goodbye! Goodbye, Mr. Skinner. Remember that I count upon that famous discussion with you. And you may rely entirely upon my discretion — in the matter of your secret, you know."

Father and daughter stood for a moment, gazing at the door behind which their noble guest had disappeared. Then the girl turned her eyes with decision upon the author of her being.

"Papa," she said, with calm resolution, "what did he intend to convey by his remarks about this secret of yours?"

"Why, Adele," the other protested, faltering a little under her look, "you yourself repudiated, in the most eloquent and unanswerable words, the bare suggestion that I could possibly be animated by the desire to cloak any unworthy deed or incident from your observation."

"That was for his benefit," she replied, tranquilly. "I was determined that he should know what we thought of his code of morals. But that does not at all affect the question of what you have been doing. Do I understand that you are going to insist on refusing to tell me where you have been, whom you have seen, what your so-called secret is about?"

"Adele!" he urged, "I really must preserve a reticence as to the essential details of the matter in question— perhaps only for a few days— at least until the obligation of secrecy is removed. You would not have me recreant to my plighted faith, would you?"

"But what business had you going and making her any such promise?"

"Her!" Mr. Skinner said, feebly smiling; "you jest, my dear Adele. How can you conceivably imagine it was a 'her'?"

"I don't imagine; I know," responded the daughter, with a hard, dry smile. "You have been seeing that yellow-haired girl that Lord Drumpipes had with him at the Museum yesterday. The letter which summoned you forth this morning was from her. You made some paltering excuses to me, and went out to meet her— and you won't look me in the eye and deny it."

In truth he did not take up her challenge. He hung his head, looked away, and shuffled with his feet. "All I am at liberty to say," he remarked at last, with visible emotion, "is that my grief at being compelled to rest temporarily under the unwelcome shadow of your suspicion is, to some slight extent, mitigated by the consciousness that when you know all you will do ample justice to the probity of my motives and the honorable character of my actions. I might even go further, and express the conviction that the outcome will be of a nature to afford you unalloyed personal satisfaction."

"That may all be," returned Adele; "but, in the meantime, you don't go out in London any more by yourself!"

Mosscrop laughed to himself as he ran down the stairs of the hotel. The spirit of mirth remained with him while he more slowly ascended the flight of steps, and the dingy passage and covered byway leading up to the Strand. It was the most comical thing he had ever heard of, and he chuckled again and again during the climb. But upon the bustling crowded thoroughfare it somehow ceased to seem so funny, or at least its value as a source of entertainment began to diminish rapidly. He found his mind reverting irresistibly to the disappointment of the early morning.

The image of Vestalia rose upon his mental vision, and would not go away. He brooded over it as he walked, and recognized that intervening incidents and personalities had in no sense dimmed his interest in it. He pictured her wonderful hair again, her bright-faced smile, her dear little airs and graces, with a yearning emptiness of heart.

The luncheon obtainable at the Barbary Club was even more unpalatable than usual, which was saying much. The familiar fact that the waiters were Germans struck him afresh, and took on the proportions of an international grievance. There were some fellows upstairs playing at what they supposed was whist. He stood for a while over the shoulders of a couple of the gamesters, and noted, with a cynical eye, the progress of their hot rivalry as to which should contribute the larger incapacity and the finer stupidity to the losing of the rubber. When they asked him if he wanted to cut in, he turned away with a snort of derisive scorn.

Over in the billiard-room there were only the marker and the member who played far worse than anybody else in the club, David sourly consented to occupy himself with this egregious outsider, and was beaten by him. The result was so clearly due to accident that he laid some money on the next game. Again the duffer fluked like mad, and won, and in a third game his luck was of such a glaring character, that Mosscrop could not refrain from loud comment. This his antagonist resented. They parted with harsh words, and Mosscrop, cursing the hour when it first occurred to him to identify himself with such a squalid pot-house, hastened angrily to shake its dust from his feet.

He made his way, by devious streets whose old book-stalls for once beckoned him in vain, to Bloomsbury and the Museum. A kind of idea had grown up unobtrusively in the background of his thoughts, that possibly he might find Vestalia there. It assumed the definite outlines of an expectation as soon as he entered the building. When he stood in the reading-room itself, and began a systematic scrutiny of its radiating rows of readers, it was with as much confidence as if he had come by appointment. The failure to discover her disturbed and annoyed him. He made a slow tour of the inner circle, then another of the broader outer ring, and suffered no one of the professed students to escape his examining eye.

What a crew they were! He had never realized it before. His hostile inspection laid bare the puerile devices of the young fools who came by concerted arrangement, took down books at random, and, sitting close together, carried on clandestine flirtations under the sightless mask of literature. He glowered with a newly-informed vision at the extraordinary females whom no one had planned to meet— the lone women with eccentric coiffures and startling costumes, who emerge from heaven knows where, and mysteriously gather here in quest of something which it seems incredible that even heaven should be able to define. Observing now the vacuous egotism of their flutterings and posturings in other people's way, the despairing clutch at public attention made by their outlandish vestiture and general get-up, David's thoughts settled grimly upon the fact that there were lands, the seats of ancient civilizations, where superfluous female children were drowned at birth. Here, he reflected, with sullen irony, we teach them to read and write, and build and stock a vast reading-room for them instead. His mood preferred the Ganges to the Thames.

There was more pathos in the spectacle of another class of habitual attendants—the poor, shabby, hungry serfs of the quotation merchant. Mosscrop knew the genus by sight, and in other times had had amusement from their contemplation. How a somber rage possessed him as he beheld them toiling unintelligently, hopelessly, under the lash of starvation. He watched one of the slave-drivers for a while, a short, red man, of swollen spiderish aspect, who moved about keeping these sweated wretches at their toil, now doling out a few pence to one who could remain erect unnourished not a minute longer, and who slunk out forthwith with a wolfish haste, now withering some other with whispered reproaches of threats. Mosscrop longed to go and break this creature's neck, or at the very least to kick him, with loud curses and utmost contumely, from the room.

He went out himself, instead, animated by a freshening spirit of resentment at the futility of existence. From sheer force of habit, he dawdled in front of shop-windows, turned over hooks and prints in one after another of his accustomed resorts for second-hand merchandise, and otherwise killed time till the dinner hour. But he did it all without any inner pretence that the process afforded him consolation.

Even when he met some fellows from the Temple, in Chancery Lane, and joined them in a series of visits to ancient bars in the vicinity, where they all stood at wearisome length, and argued with intolerable inconsequence about wholly irrelevant matters over their drinks, his thoughts maintained a moody concentration upon the theme of his personal unhappiness. The stray contributions which he offered to the general conversation were all of an acrid, not to say truculent, character. He had a sort of dour satisfaction in the utterance of offensive gibes and bitter jokes. Twice the threat of an altercation arose, in consequence of these ill-natured comments of his, and David sullenly welcomed the imminent quarrel; but the intervention of the others, without any help from him, cleared the atmosphere again.

Even the peacemakers, however, evinced the opinion that he was behaving badly, and nodded cheerful adieus when at last he declared that they were a parcel of uninspired loons, with whom he marveled to find himself consuming valuable time. They lifted their glasses at him mockingly as he strode away, with the gleam of an unexpressed "good riddance!" in their eyes.

The consciousness that he had made himself disagreeable to these fellows had its uses as a counter-irritant to his inner self-disgust. It rendered solitude at least a trifle more supportable. He bought a novel, and read it beside his plate at Simpson's, where the heavy joints and weighty old ale just fitted his mood.

The book was one which the papers were talking of for the moment. David reflected grimly as he skimmed the opening chapters that Vestalia had asked him why he didn't write a Scotch novel. They were all the vogue, she said, and while the fashion lasted, it was nonsense for any Scotchman to pretend that he could not profitably occupy his leisure time. He had replied, with some flippancy, that his imaginative powers might compass the construction of a tale, hut were unequal to the task of inventing also a whole dialect to tell it in.

How, as the whim returned to him, his fancy parodied a title for this unborn work. How would "A Goddess, Some Merely Ordinary Fools and Lord Drumpipes" do?

Ah! that Drumpipes! David paid his bill, lit a cigar, and sallied forth, suddenly informed with the notion of going to the Inn, and having it out with the Earl. He doubled up his fists as he hurried along.

The top floor at Dunstan's was wrapped in darkness. Mosscrop knocked and kicked first at "Mr. Linkhaw's" door to make sure that no one was in, then opened his own, and struck a light. The apartment wore still in his eyes the chill desolation of aspect which he remembered from the morning.

There had been a change in the weather, and the suggestion of a fire was in the damp air. He put on his loose jacket and slippers, recalling sadly as he did so the vision he had beheld only twenty-four hours before, of that pretty little ermined footgear on the fender beside his, in front of the glowing grate. He brought out the decanter and a glass, and sighed deeply.

Then all at once he caught sight of something white in the letter box. In the same instant he was tearing open a stamped envelope, addressed in a large, strange hand which yet he knew so well, and excitedly striving to gulp in the meaning of the whole written page before him, without troubling to read the lines in their sequence. Yes, it was from her, and—yes, it contained words of kindness and even of tenderness which shone brilliantly forth here and there from the context. He pulled himself together, and walking over to the light, began resolutely at the beginning.

"Dear Mr. Mosscrop,—I hope you were not very much disappointed at finding me gone this morning, or rather, I hope you were a little disappointed, but will not be so any longer when you get this explanation. I don't know either that it can be called an explanation, for it doesn't seem to me that I am at all able to explain even to myself, much less to you.

"The fact is that you were so kind and so sweet to me, that I simply had to do what I have done. I saw it all, after we had parted. Under the circumstances, and especially considering the delicate and noble manner in which you had treated me, it was the only thing I could do!

"I should have left a message for you in your letter-box, but there was not a scrap of paper, not even a book out of which I could tear a fly-leaf, in Mr. Linkhaw's room, nor writing materials of any sort. I have bought this paper at the stationer's, and am writing this note in an hotel writing-room.

"The dear dressing-bag, and the other beautiful things which I owe to you, I took away with me because it would have broken my heart to leave them, and I felt sure you would be glad to have me take them. Every time I look at them, and all other times too, I shall think of the best man I ever knew or dreamed of. Something very important has occurred, which may turn out to be of the greatest possible advantage to me. It is very uncertain as yet, and I cannot tell you about it at present, but soon I hope to be able to do so.

"In the meantime, please believe in my undying gratitude. Vestalia."

David drew a long breath, poured a drink for himself, lit his pipe, and sat down to read the letter all over again. He arrived slowly at the conclusion that he was glad she had written it—but beyond that his sensations remained obstinately undefined.

The girl had disappeared behind a thick high wall which his imagination was unequal to the task of surmounting. A few stray facts assumed a certain distinctness in his mind: she had evidently gone off quite of her own accord, and she had appreciated the spirit of his attitude towards her the previous day, and she had encountered on this, the following day, something or somebody which might bring her good luck. What kind of good luck? he wondered.

There was an implied promise in her words that he should be informed when this mysterious beneficence assumed shape. This had very little comfort in it for him. In fact, he found he rather hated the idea of her enjoying good luck in which he had no share.

Suppose instead that it didn't come off. Would she return to him then, or at least let him know, so that he might hasten forward again as her special providence?

Ah, that is what he had wanted to be—her providence. The notion of doing everything for her, of being the source of all she had, of foreseeing her wants, inventing her pleasures, ministering joyfully to the least of her sweet little caprices—the charm of this role fascinated him more than ever.

He recalled in detail the emotions of delight he had experienced in buying things for her. By some law which he recognized without analyzing, the greatest pleasure had arisen from the purchase of the articles which she needed most. There had been only a moderate and tempered ecstasy in paying for champagne, but oh, the bliss of buying her boots, and those curling-irons, and the comb! He thrilled again with it, in retrospect. What would it have been to see her clad entirely in garments of his providing?

But the cage was empty—the bird had flown. Would she come back again? Was there really the remotest hint of such a possibility in her letter?

No. He read it still again, and shook his head at the fender with a despairing groan. The gloom of his reverie benumbed his senses. He let his pipe go out, and suffered the glass at his elbow to remain untouched, as he sat with his sad thoughts for company, and did not even hear the footsteps which presently ascended the stairs.

A soft little knock at the door startled him from his meditations. He stood up, with his heart fluttering, and lifted his hand in wonderment to his brow. Had he been asleep and dreaming?

The dainty tapping on the panel renewed itself. David moved as in a trance toward the door.

Chapter 9

Mosscrop turned the spring-lock noiselessly, and drew the door open with caressing gentleness. His eyes had intuitively prepared themselves to discern the slender form of Vestalia in the dim light of the passage. They beheld instead, with bewildered repulsion, a burly masculine bulk. Wandering upward in angry confusion from the level on which they had expected her dear face, they took in the fatuous, moon-like visage of Lord Drumpipes.

"Dear God!" groaned David, in frank abandonment to disgust.

"I came up quietly this time," said the Earl. "You made such a row about my being noisy last night, I thought to myself, 'Now, anything to please Davie! I'll steal up like a mouse in list-slippers.'"

David scowled angry impatience at him. "Who the deuce cares what you do?" he demanded, roughly. "You might have marched up with a Salvation Army band, for all it matters to me."

"Ah," said Drumpipes, placidly pushing his way past Mosscrop through the open door. "Well, give me a drink, Davie, man, and then tell me all about it. Where may the lady be at the present moment?"

Mosscrop came in, and produced another glass with a gloomy air. He watched the Earl seat himself in the biggest chair and help himself from the decanter, and light his pipe, all in moody silence. "She's gone away," he said at last, coldly.

"And a good job, too!" remarked the other. "Distrust all yellow-hair, Davie! Have you been in my place and seen what that woman did? There was my Athabaska moose actually torn from the wall, and pulled to bits on the floor! It's a matter of fifty shillings, or even more, Davie. Considering what you'd already spent on her, I call that heartless behavior on her part. She must be a bad sort indeed to take all you would give her, and fool you to the top of your bent, and then wantonly destroy property that she knew you'd have to make good, before she took French leave. Ah, women are not given that kind of hair for nothing! You're well out of a thankless mess, Davie."

Mosscrop looked musingly at his friend. He smiled a little to himself, and then sighed as well.

A calmer temper returned to him. "I don't take your view of it, Archie," he said, almost gently. "I have been as sad about it as a child who's lost its pet, but I'm less disconsolate than I was. Some compensations occur to me—and besides, I have a letter from her. It came tonight, and from its tone——"

"Burn it, man, burn it!" the other adjured him, with eager fervor. "Drive the whole business from your mind! If you'll give me your solemn word, Davie, not to see her again"—the Earl paused, to invest his further words with a deeper gravity—"if you'll promise faithfully to have no more to do with her, I'll forgive you the moose. I said fifty shillings, but I doubt your getting a good job much under three pounds. Well, then, if you say the word, I'll pocket that loss. Hang it all, you're my boyhood friend, and I'd go to a considerable length to save you from a dangerous entanglement of this sort. Although it was by no means an ordinary head. Man, I fair loved that moosie!"

Mosscrop's smooth-shaven and somewhat sallow visage had gradually lost its melancholy aspect. A cheerful grin began now to play about the corners of his mouth.

"Archie," he said with an affectation of exaggerated seriousness, "a moose more or less is not worth mentioning by comparison with the situation which is about to confront you. I know the particular beast you speak of. It was not up to much. The fur was dropping out in patches on its neck, one of its eyes was loose, and the red paint on the nostrils was oxidized. You would not have got twelve-and-six for it anywhere in the world. But if it had been the choicest trophy that was ever mounted, and then its value were multiplied a hundred-fold, it would still be a waste of your time to give it a second thought. Graver matters demand your attention, Archie."

The Earl's countenance lengthened, and he set down his glass. He apparently did not trust himself to speak, but stared in alarmed inquiry at his friend.

"As you said a while ago," pursued David, with vexatious deliberation, "we have been pals from boyhood. My father was your grandfather's man of business, and was your factor till his death. You and I played together before we were breeched. We went to school together, and I spent more holidays at Skirl with you than I did at home. So I know the ins and outs of your family and its affairs practically as well as you do. I know your sisters ——"

"You don't mean that Ellen has given up her Zenana mission work in Burmah, and returned here to England?" Drumpipes interposed, with a convulsive catch in his breath.

"No; the Lady Ellen, so far as I know, is still peacefully occupied in harrowing up the domestic life of the Orient in her well-known and most effective manner."

"Well, anything else must be a minor evil," said the Earl, with an accent of relief. "Whichever of the rest of them it is, Davie, I tell you at the outset that I wash my hands of the business. My sisters rendered the first twenty-five years of my life a torment upon earth. They bullied me out of all peace in life as a youngster; they made my rotten marriage for me; they took my money and then blackened my character in reward; they——"

"Oh, I know all those gags by heart," interposed Mosscrop. "They're really very decent bodies, those sisters of yours; if they had a fault, it was in believing that they could make a silk purse out of a sow's ear. But it's not about them at all that I was speaking. The point is, Archie, that I have made the acquaintance of Mr. Laban Skinner and his extremely attractive daughter."

The Earl took in this intelligence with ponderous slowness. He sipped at his glass in silence, and then stared for a little at his friend. "Well, what is there so alarming about that?" he demanded at last, roughening his voice in puzzled annoyance. "They're respectable people, aren't they? And what the deuce are you driving at, anyway?"

"Ah, if you take that tone with me, old man, I pull out of the affair at once."

Drumpipes scowled. "What affair? How do you know there is any affair! And what business have you got being in it, if there is an affair? You're over-officious, my friend. You take too much on yourself."

Mosscrop laughed with tantalizing enjoyment in his eyes. "Confess that you think of making a Countess of the lady."

"Well, and what if I do?" the Earl retorted. "Damn it all, man, I haven't to ask your leave, have I? And, come now, I put it to you straight, have you ever seen a finer woman in your life?"

David lifted his brows judicially, and held his head to one side. "Oh, I'm not saying she's amiss—in externals," he admitted.

"Man, she's wonderful! Just wonderful!" cried the other. "Did you mind her walk? It is as if she'd never been outside a palace in her life. And the face, the eyes, the color, the figure—what Queen in Europe can match them? Man, since I first laid eyes on her, I've not been myself at all. The thought of her bewitches me. I hardly know what I'm doing. I've been today to my tailor's, and I gave him orders that fair took his breath away. The most expensive clothes, and even furs, I ordered with as light a heart as if it were a matter of sixpences. The man knows me from childhood, and he gazed at me as if I was clean daft. He was shaking his head to himself when I came away. Oh, I'm quite a different person, I assure you. I literally hurl money about me, nowadays."

"You must indeed be in love," said Mosscrop. "The father—he gives one the notion of a man of wealth."

The Earl's face glistened. "He's in the Standard Oil Company!" he whispered, impressively.

This fact created an atmosphere of dignified solemnity for itself. The two men looked at each other gravely for a while, saying nothing. Then the Earl, with a contemplative air, refilled his glass.

"She is the most beautiful woman I've ever known," he said, earnestly; "and I think she will marry me."

"Physical beauty and Standard Oil do make an alluring combination," remarked David philosophically; "but——"

"Oh, there are no 'buts,'" Drumpipes insisted. "She's as fine in mind and temper as she is in body. I'm very particular about intellect, as you know, and I've studied her closely. She has a very sound brain, Davie— for a woman. But how on earth did you come to stumble upon them?"

Mosscrop did not explain. "The thing that impressed me about her, curiously enough," he said, with tranquil discursiveness, "was her extremely democratic aversion to our ranks and hereditary titles. She and her father seem to be the most violent anti-aristocrats I ever knew."

"Yes, that is a trifle awkward," the Earl admitted. "I don't think it's more than skin-deep with the old man, but Adele— that's her name, as beautiful as herself, isn't it?— she's tremendously in earnest about it. That has rather queered my pitch— I haven't told them, you know, about the title and all that. They know me just as simple Mr. Linkhaw."

"'Simple' is so precisely the word," commented Mosscrop.

"Well, what was I to do?" the other protested in self-defense. "I was traveling under that name in Kentucky—went there to look at a big sale of thoroughbreds, you know— and met the father, and then I met the girl, and they had me to their house in the country — a magnificent place, by George— and she had so much to say against the classes here, and took such a strong position against titles and all that— why, I would have been a juggins to tell her at the start; and after, it gradually occurred to me that I wouldn't say anything at all, but just go on and win her as plain Mr.

Linkhaw. Then I could be sure I was being loved for myself alone, couldn't I?"

"Your sentimentality is most touching," said David; "but I fear it will cost you heavily."

"Oh, by the way, yes," remarked Drumpipes, collecting his thoughts; "you said something awhile ago about there being a bother of some sort. What is it?" Then an idea occurred to him, and he lifted his head eagerly. "You haven't gone and blabbed about me, have you— told her who I was, and all that?"

"Quite the contrary," smiled David. "It was she who recognized me at once as the Earl of Drumpipes. It seems you showed her my picture on shipboard, and told her who I was, and all about me. Do you recall the incident?"

The Earl nodded, foolishly. "It's my confounded imagination," he groaned. "I'm always making an ass of myself like that. God only knows why I should have gone out of my way to invent that idiotic rubbish. But you get awfully bard up for conversation on shipboard, you know. And so it all came out, and she's chuckling to think what a clumsy liar and guy I made of myself— and I've gone and ordered all those clothes— and——"

"Be reassured, most noble Thane," cried David, gaily. "There has been no disclosure. Nothing came out. I accepted the situation. I did not for an instant betray you. I said, 'Certainly: I am the Earl of Drumpipes,' without so much as the flicker of an eyelid. There's friendship for you, if you like."

"And did she believe—" the Earl began to ask. Then he choked with rising mirth, gasped, rolled about in his chair, and finally burst forth in resounding laughter. "She thinks you— you"— he started out again, and once more went off in loud merriment. "It's the funniest thing I ever heard of," he murmured at last, restoring his composure with difficulty, and grinning at Mosscrop through eyes wet with joyful tears.

"It delights me to see how keenly the humorous aspect of the matter appeals to you," observed David, "because there is another phase of it which may seem to be deficient in gaiety."

"No; you as the Earl, that's too funny!" persisted Drumpipes, with a fresh outbreak of laughter. But this somehow rang a little false at the finish. A half-doubtful look came into his eyes, and sobered his countenance. "But you'll stand by me in this thing, old man, now that you've begun it, won't you?" he asked, in an altered tone.

"But I didn't begin it," David pointed out calmly. "You began it yourself, and she took it up of her own accord. I've simply sacrificed myself in your interest. I stood still, and heard my motives aspersed, my character vilified, my objects in life covered with contumely, all on account of your hereditary crimes, and took it all like a lamb. But to assume that I'm going to do this again, or indefinitely, is another matter. I don't mind submitting to a single temporary humiliation for a friend's sake, but to make a profession of it is too much. If it were even a decent full-blown peerage it might be different, but to be traduced for nothing better than a Scotch title— no, thank you!"

"You're not the friend I took you for," commented the Earl, in depressed tones. "For that matter," he added, defiantly, "we were Pilliewillies in Slug-Angus before the Campbells were ever heard of, or the Gordons had learnt not to eat their cattle raw. And no Linkhaw has ever said to a Mosscrop, 'I see you're in a hole and I'll leave you there.'"

David smiled. "No, you would always give a hand— for a fixed price. Well, Archie, I'm not saying I won't see you through all this, but there must be conditions. And there must be a plan. What on earth do you intend to do?"

"Well, my idea is," the other answered, hesitatingly, "that I should ask her to be my wife while she still supposes I am merely Mr. Linkhaw. She is like all American girls in this, that she believes entirely in love matches. So if she will marry me as Mr. Linkhaw, it will signify that she loves me. Very well then, that being the case, I can say to her afterward that I ventured upon a trifling deception, solely to have the chance to win the woman I wanted, and to make sure that I was being loved for myself alone. And then, hang it all, I don't believe it lies in any woman's skin to be angry at finding that she's been made a countess unawares. If I said I was an Earl and turned out not to be one, then she'd have a grievance, but it's the other way about."

"Precisely," put in David, "that particular ignominy is reserved for me. But suppose she doesn't accept you."

"That's hardly worth supposing. It's as good as understood between us, I think, that she will accept me."

"But then suppose she jilts you, after you disclose to her that you are not plain Mr. Linkhaw."

"If that's well managed, I'm not afraid of it, either. You see, her father's not an out-and-out American. He was really born in England, and went out there as a boy. That's a very curious thing, you know. Englishmen who go there, and like the place, get to be more American than the Yankees are themselves. But they don't change their blood, do they? And women are pretty much alike, too, whatever their blood may be. They're all organized to stand a coronet on the corner of their pocket handkerchiefs. No, it'll be all right, if only you stay by me."

"Ah, now we come to realities," said Mosscrop, genially. "It'll be rather an expensive business, Archie. I have very high notions, my friend, as to the scale on which an Earl should comport himself. I could not dream of doing the thing on the thrifty and contracted basis which suits you. The task is a difficult one to me. I shall have to sit and look entirely devoid of mental sensations of any sort for hours at a time. I know nothing of football and cricket, and have not the name of a single jockey on my tongue; this will render conversation an embarrassing matter for me. I shall suffer continually from the knowledge that I am being regarded as a vicious fool, a rake, a gambler, and libertine of the most heartless description, and this will wear a good deal on my nerves. Compensation of some sort I must have. Now, I entertain the theory that a nobleman should never have any small change about him at all. Tips to waiters I would make a great point of. They should invariably be of gold. To slip a sovereign into a hall-porter's hand is also a valuable action. His subsequent demeanor gives the cue to the attitude of the whole visible world toward you. A four-in-hand to Brighton is good substantial form, too, if enough pains be taken with the outfit. A private hansom in town is, of course, indispensable. I realize, Archie," he concluded apologetically, "that I am not displaying a specially comprehensive grasp of the requirements of rank. I can only think of a few things now, on the spur of the moment; but I will concentrate all my energies on the task once I take it up in earnest. You may trust me to rise to the occasion. I will be a nobleman that mere baronets will turn round in the street to look after."

Drumpipes exhibited a wan and troubled smile. "You'd have your joke, Davie, out of any man's distress," he said, weakly.

"Joke!" cried Mosscrop. "You make an awful error there, Archie. Never was man more serious."

"But there would be no opportunity for you to spend money, or display yourself," urged the other. "Not, of course, that I would begrudge a pound or two, more or less, if there were a real need of it. But in this case, the whole point is that you should lie low, and not be seen any more. There is no necessity that she should meet you again. In fact, the more I think of it, the clearer it is that she shouldn't. It might spoil everything, don't you see?"

"Oh no, my lad!" rejoined David, cheerfully. "I'm not of the hermit variety of aristocrat. I'm the kind of Earl who's on the spot, and who lets people know that he is present. I will have rings on my fingers and bells on my toes. I will— why, let me see!"

His face brightened at some wandering thought. "Why, man, I have a birthday in six days' time! That's it, the 24th. I knew there was the difference of a year lacking a week between us. She read it to me this morning out of the peerage—August 24th. Very well, then, I will celebrate the anniversary as it has never been celebrated before. I will provide an entertainment for my immediate friends upon a scale befitting my position and the importance of the event commemorated. What do you think of a special saloon-carriage to Portsmouth, and a dinner on my yacht, eh? One could be hired and manned for the occasion, and a staff of cooks and servants sent down from an hotel here. Or could you get them in Portsmouth? Does anything more appropriate occur to you?"

"Go on with your jest," replied the other, sullenly. "All I can say is, it's in damned bad taste, though. Here I am in this predicament, and you pour vinegar into my wounds instead of oil."

"Standard Oil, I assume that you refer to. No, you shall have the oil, Archie. You shall be my guest on the occasion, and you shall meet Mr. and Miss Skinner. We four will constitute the party; and I will provide such an engaging spectacle of the nobleman, the bearer of hereditary dignities and titles, seen close at hand among his intimate friends, that the lady will be moved to admiration. She will say, 'Ah, I never guessed before how delightful an Earl could be, how perfect in manners, how admirable in tact, how superb in his capacity as host.' I will reconcile her to the aristocracy en bloc."

"Say, you know," interposed Drumpipes, "I'm not sure there isn't something in that."

"Something in it? My dear sir, it's rammed with fructifying probabilities. I give this party, and I do it as an Earl should do things. I exert myself to fascinate this transatlantic twain. I lead their imaginations captive to my hereditary seductiveness. I make them feel that to be the guests of an Earl is more than beauty and fine raiment and Standard Oil. I excite them to a warm glow of tenderness toward feudalism, a mood that melts at mere thought of the medieval. At that psychological moment you jump in and intimate that you're something of an Earl yourself—and there you are!"

Drumpipes nodded approving comprehension, while he pondered the project thus outlined. "I'm not sure I don't like the scheme," he repeated. "It's risky, though. She's fearfully keen of scent, that girl is. If you didn't play it for all you were worth, every minute, she'd twig the thing like a shot. You'd leave her with me a good deal, wouldn't you, and devote yourself to the old man? That would be the safest, you know."

"That would hardly do. It wouldn't be in character. When an Earl is giving a party, and there is a beautiful young woman about, he doesn't go and talk with windy old fossils in frock-coats. It would look unnatural. It might as like as not excite suspicion. And now you'd better clear out. I want to go to bed."

The Earl rose, stood irresolute for a moment, and then put a hand on Mosscrop's shoulder. "Davie," he said gravely, "there's one thing you must remember. You're not a good man to handle money—if I didn't know your forbears, I'd never credit your being a Scot at all— remember, laddie, that those lawyers have run up terrible bills against me, and farm values have all dropped in the most fearful fashion, and I've not kept so tight a hand on the purse-strings of late, myself, as usual, and so do this thing as moderately——"

"Oh, you be damned!" laughed Mosscrop, and pushed him from the room.

When he was alone, the notion of going to bed seemed to have lost its urgency. He lighted his pipe, and sat down to read Vestalia's letter once again.

Chapter 10

At breakfast, three mornings later, Mr. Laban Skinner and his daughter dallied over their plates, and sent the waiter out again with some asperity when he, taking it for granted they must have finished the meal, came in to clear the table.

Each had been reading a letter, from the early morning mail.

"It is an invitation from the Earl of Drumpipes," remarked the father, regarding his daughter over his pince-nez, "expressing, in what I am constrained to describe as somewhat abrupt and common-place terms, his desire that we should consider ourselves as his guests during the entire day upon the approaching 24th instant, the occasion being the anniversary of his birth." He handed over the note for her inspection as he spoke. "The impression which his phraseology produces upon me," he added, "is that of one performing a perfunctory act of courtesy to foreigners of his acquaintance, to whom he extends the ceremonial proffer of a hospitality which he assumes will be declined."

"Oh, not at all, papa," commented Adele, briefly glancing at the note. "All noblemen write in that formal way. It is a part of their bringing-up. No; he wants us to come, right enough. I have a letter here from Mr. Linkhaw, explaining the thing. Of course it was a suggestion of his."

"I venture the hope," said Mr. Skinner, "that he improves the opportunity to also explain the otherwise unintelligible fact that during an entire week we have had neither ocular evidence nor any other tangible manifestation of his presence upon this side of the Atlantic. I do not hesitate to avow my surprise at what, after his manifold and, I might say, even importunate professions of eagerness to place his services at our disposal in London, I find myself unable to refrain from regarding as his indifference to our — our being here."

"No," said Adele, confidently, "it's all right. He was kept longer in Scotland than he expected— very urgent family business of some sort— and only arrived in London a couple of days ago, and has been up to his eyes in work since he came. Besides," she continued with a little smile, "he is very frank; he says he has no clothes fit to go about in London with, but his tailor is working at some new ones for him day and night, and they are promised for the 23d, so that at the birthday party next day——"

"I am far from presuming, Adele," interrupted the father, gravely, "to ascribe to you a deficiency or obtuseness of perception where considerations of delicacy are involved; but I think I am warranted in pointing out that at home, at least in the social environment to which you have been from your infancy accustomed, a young gentleman would intuitively eschew a subject of this nature in his correspondence with a young lady."

"Oh, they're different here," explained the daughter, with nonchalance. "They talk quite openly over here of lots of things which we never dream of mentioning. You remember that lady in front of us at the theater last night— when the men in their dress suits came over to talk with her between the acts— how she told them right out, that although it was so hot she had to fan herself all the while, still her legs felt quite shivery. Now, a speech like that would stand Louisville on its head, let alone Paris, Kentucky, but here it passes without the slightest notice. It's the custom of the country. I rather like it myself."

Mr. Skinner sighed, and pecked timorously at his egg with a spoon. "I am not wanting, I trust, in tolerance for the natural divergences of habit and manner which distinguish the widely-separated branches of the Anglo-Saxon race, or in a desire to accommodate myself to their peculiarities when I confront them in the course of foreign travel; but I with difficulty bring myself to contemplate with satisfaction the method of partaking of a soft-boiled egg which obtains favor in these islands. To my mind, the negation of the principle of a center of gravity involved in the construction of this egg cup, combined with the objectionably inadequate dimensions of the spoon——"

"Dig it out on to your plate, then; the waiter won't come in again till I ring," suggested the daughter.

"I prefer the alternative of abstention," he answered. "The spectacle of stains upon the cloth or upon the plate would be equally suggestive to the servant's scrutiny."

He rose as he spoke. Adele, gathering up the letters, did likewise, and rang the bell.

Mr. Skinner, having glanced out at the river panorama from the balcony window for a little, and then looked over the market columns of a newspaper, turned again to his daughter.

"I gather that we are to accept the invitation of the Earl of Drumpipes," he remarked, tentatively.

Adele nodded. "Why, of course," she said; "that's to be the formal beginning of everything. It is intended to make our position here perfectly regular. Lord Drumpipes is the head of Mr. Linkhaw's family. It is entirely becoming that he should take the initiative in recognizing us."

"Ah yes, in recognizing us," he repeated. "I suppose, Adele, it would be futile for me to recur to the question whether you have sufficiently weighed the opposing considerations with regard to Mr. Linkhaw, and the——"

"Mercy, yes!" interposed Adele, with promptitude. "Don't let's have that all over again. I've quite settled everything in my own mind."

"Since I was afforded the opportunity of personally observing and conversing with the Earl of Drumpipes," pursued the father, "and of thus forming authoritative conclusions as to the British nobility in general, I have devoted much thought to the subject. While I do not suggest that my well-known views upon the aristocratic institution, as a whole, have undergone any perceptible transformation, I do not shrink from the admission that the thought of being connected by marriage with the bearer of an hereditary title no longer presents itself to me in such repulsive colors as was formerly the case. If, therefore, with your undoubted advantages, it should occur to you to entertain the idea of a possible alliance with the nobility, I would not have you feel that my convictions formed a necessarily insuperable barrier to——".

"No, no!" the daughter broke in, with a laugh. "I'll promise to disregard your convictions as much as you like. But now I want you to go out, and kill time by yourself somewhere till luncheon. I want to be left alone. There is some place where elderly American gentlemen can go, isn't there, without getting into mischief? Oh yes, you must go, and not just downstairs to hang about the hotel entrance, but straight away somewhere. Why? My dear papa, I have my secrets as well as you."

"But that secret of mine," he protested feebly, "I assure you, Adele, that it is really nothing at all. That is, it does involve matters both interesting and important; but the fact that I am precluded from mentioning them is in the nature of a pure accident, and wholly without significance."

"Goodbye till luncheon time," answered Adele, with affable firmness. "And mind you quit the premises."

Mr. Skinner found his hat, smiled dubiously at his daughter, and without further parley took himself off.

Adele, left alone, looked at the watch in her girdle, and compared its record with that of the ornate clock on the mantel. She took up the paper and ran an aimless eye over one page after another. Then she walked about with a restless movement, pausing from time to time to bend a frowning yet indifferent inspection upon the scene spread out beyond the balcony.

At last there came a tap on the door, and at sound of this, even as she called out a clear, commanding "Come!" she withdrew all signs of perturbation, or of emotion of any sort, from her beautiful dark countenance.

It was Vestalia who entered the room— Vestalia, clad in daintily unpretentious and becoming garments, neatly gloved, and with much radiant self-possession upon her pretty face.

She paused upon the threshold, nodded rather than bowed to her hostess, and let a little smile sparkle in her eyes and play about her rosebud of a mouth.

"Your father does not succeed very well in keeping his secrets, I observe," she remarked, pleasantly, by way of an overture to conversation.

"Won't you please to be seated," said Adele, with exaggerated calmness. She herself took a chair, and slowly surveyed her visitor as she went on: "My father has no secrets from me. He tries to have— once in a blue moon— but it doesn't come off. I may tell you frankly, however, that he has in this case told me nothing. I found your address, and other information, in looking through his pockets. I am under no obligation to tell you this: I simply feel like it, that's all. I hate dissimulation."

"And I suppose you have your things made up without pockets," suggested Vestalia, amiably.

Adele put some added resolution into her glance. "I wrote asking you to call," she said coldly, "because it became a nuisance not to know what you were up to."

"Ah," replied Vestalia, "it looks as if your father must have destroyed some of our correspondence. How thoughtless of him!"

Miss Skinner paused, and knitted her queenly brows a trifle. She did not seem to be getting on. "I have no wish to waste time in trying to be funny," she avowed, after some hesitation. "Now that you are here, have you any objection to telling me why you swore my father to keep a secret from me?"

"Oh, just a whim of mine, nothing more," Vestalia assured her, lightly. "I frequently have notions like that, that I can't in the least account for."

"No, you had a reason," insisted the other, with gravity. "And you must tell me what it was. I have been frank with you."

"And I will not be behind you in candor," said Vestalia, as if won by an appeal to her better self. "It was because you looked at me in the Museum as if you thought my hair was dyed."

"Well, so it is, isn't it?" demanded Adele, bluntly.

"Upon my honor, no!" the other replied. "And now you look at me as if you thought that that wasn't much to swear by. It's possible that you do not realize it, but your eyes leave something to be desired in the matter of politeness."

"I'm afraid that's true," Adele assented. "I have an effect of looking very hard at things, simply because I'm near-sighted. I ought to wear glasses, but they do not suit me."

"Yes," said Vestalia, with a meditative look, "it would be a pity for you to put them on. They would detract from your face. It is very beautiful as it is— for a dark style."

"Sometimes I feel that I am almost tired of being dark," confessed Adele. "Your hair is the most wonderful thing I ever saw. I could see that your gentleman-friend at the Museum admired it immensely."

"Oh yes, he said so repeatedly," Vestalia replied, with a demure display of pleasure at the recollection.

Again there was a little pause. Then Miss Skinner essayed another opening. "Your name— Peaussier— would indicate French extraction," she remarked. "And French people are so very dark, as a rule, aren't they? My mother was a Creole— from Louisiana, you know— and I suppose that accounts for my color."

"Well, my mother was Scotch," explained Vestalia, "and they are sandy."

"The Scotch gentleman that you were with at the Museum— he was decidedly a dark man," suggested Adele, with a casual manner.

"Now that I think of it, so he was," said Vestalia.

The measured and ceremonious ticking of the expensive clock on the mantel had the silence to itself for a space, while the two ladies looked at each other.

"So you won't tell me anything?" Miss Skinner exclaimed at last.

"The trouble is, don't you see, that I am quite in the dark as to what you want to know. If you will tell me just what was in your father's pockets, I can judge then what gaps exist in your information."

Adele laughed aloud. "I believe you are really a tip-top good fellow, in spite of everything," she declared. "Do tell me what it is you are doing! I assure you you're utterly wrong in thinking that I am a person to guard against, to keep secrets from. Come, don't you see how much I really like you? And you won't trust me! I suppose it is the blonde temperament, suspicious and unresponsive and calculating. Or no, I don't mean that, you know I don't, but you might repose more confidence in me, when I have told you everything."

"Everything?" murmured Vestalia, sweetly.

"About papa's pockets, you know."

"Ah, yes."

"It was all your fault," urged Adele. "It was you who drove me to it. And if you don't tell now, goodness only knows what crimes I may not be driven to commit, in addition."

"Let me hasten to avert this awful catastrophe," cried Vestalia. "The matter is simplicity itself. I am by profession, trade, whatever you call it, a tracer of pedigrees, genealogies. I served my apprenticeship under an American lady, who worked entirely for American customers. She is dead now, and the business is broken up, and I have been idle for a long time. When I saw your father and heard his name, a thought occurred to me. I know a good deal about the Skinners in England."

"Papa was born in England himself, you know," interposed Adele, with rising interest.

"Yes, I know," Vestalia went on. "As I said, I have exceptional sources of information about the family, and it occurred to me that very likely he would be glad to have the records searched, and a full pedigree drawn up. I wrote to him, accordingly— he had mentioned this hotel— and I came and saw him downstairs in the reception-room, and he seemed delighted with the idea, and gave me a commission at once. What was more important still, he was kind enough to pay me something in advance. It came just at the moment to— to supply a very urgent want, too, I can tell you."

"Ah, poor girl!" said Adele, tenderly. "But why on earth were you afraid that I should know? I don't believe your story about the hair, you know."

"Really it was that," protested Vestalia. "I could see that you didn't like me. I was afraid of you— that is, of your prejudicing your father against me. And if you only knew how desperately I was in need of the job! Don't you remember, you did look very sharply at me."

"If I did, it was because I was surprised to—to— see who you were with."

"How do you mean?" queried Vestalia, puzzled. "We were both entire strangers to you, surely."

"No. I recognized the gentleman from a picture I had seen of him. I had a kind of idea that he was not precisely a nice gentleman for you to be with."

"Then you had a preposterous and wickedly mistaken kind of idea," said Vestalia, with decision. "There isn't a truer or nobler-spirited gentleman on this earth than he is. I have reason to know what I say. If anybody has told you otherwise, you have been lied to, that's all."

"Dear, dear, how much you are in earnest," cried Adele. "You must be my friend, and defend me behind my back like that, too. If he liked your hair immensely, why, so do I."

"Don't let us joke about him," put in Vestalia, with seriousness. "I feel very keenly about my obligation to him. He saved my life— and—and I'd rather talk about something else. We were speaking of the Skinners— and their pedigree."

Adele assented, with an inclination of the head, to the diversion, though her eyes retained their gleam of surprised curiosity. "Yes, the Skinners," she said, vaguely.

"I can trace them up to Sir Theobald Skinner, Knight, who obtained a grant of the Abbey lands of Coggesthorpe, Suffolk, in 1541— who in turn was the grandfather of Walter Skinner, who married Elizabeth, daughter and co-heir of John Banstock, Esquire, of Meechy, Norfolk, and became first Lord Gunser."

Adele pricked up her ears. "What is that? Are we related to the nobility? Oh, that is what papa meant by something interesting and important! Who would have supposed he could be so sly? Oh, sure enough, that would account for——" She broke off short, and smiled, first knowingly to herself, then with frank cordiality to Vestalia. "Oh, go on," she urged. "Tell me about our lords."

Vestalia shook her head. "We— that is, you have no lords nowadays," she admitted, ruefully. "The Gunser peerage became extinct in the male line nearly two hundred years ago. The collateral branches of the family sank to be yeomen on the soil their ancestors had owned— some of them became even peasants, agricultural laborers. There are no prosperous or polite Skinners nowadays— except your immediate branch."

"And even I haven't got polite eyes," laughed Adele. "Yes, I remember papa telling how poor his people were. He hardly knew the taste of meat, he said, till he went to America as a boy. And so you have traced all his relations out. Are there any cousins or near connections living now, do you know? He had a brother older than himself, Abram was his name, I fancy, and he enlisted in the army and went to the dogs, I think. At least, father never heard of him afterward."

"He is dead," Vestalia re-assured her. "He did go to the dogs, as you say. He had some sons, but they are dead too."

"And so there were actually Skinners in the peerage!" mused Adele, aloud. The thought seemed to excite her. She rose and looked at herself in the mirror, over Vestalia's head. The latter stood up as well.

"Oh, must you be going?" said Adele. "There was so much I wanted to say to you. We must meet soon again. I am going to insist upon that. You see, I know absolutely no one over here of my own sex, except you. It will be different in a few days, now, but that won't make any difference with my liking you. Oh, yes— I wanted to ask you— do you know a Mr. Linkhaw?"

Vestalia looked blankly at her interrogator for a moment, then flushed a little and smiled confusedly. "I have heard the name," she replied, "but I have never seen the gentleman bearing it."

Adele drew her brows together in a half-frown. "He is a great friend of the gentleman who was with you at the Museum," she said, doubtingly.

"Yes, I gathered that," answered Vestalia. "It was in that way that I heard the name."

"Really, how curiously we two are mixed up together!" cried the other, with dawning impatience. "You could tell me ever so many things that I am dying to know, if you only chose to. It is provoking to have to grope about in the dark like this. And you won't even get vexed with me, and talk back. Even that way I might learn something— and we could make it up afterward, as easy as not."

"Ah, but that is what I came resolved under no circumstances to do," explained Vestalia, with affable placidity. "Nothing would tempt me to get vexed with you."

"Suppose I insisted upon talking unpleasantly about the gentleman at the Museum," suggested Adele, with potential malice in her tone.

"I don't say you can't grieve me and hurt me, but you can't make me angry with you. You see, I know things which you don't know, which would entirely alter your views about me, and about other matters, if you were aware of them. So it would be unfair in me to blame you for remarks made in ignorance of the truth."

"But it is precisely against this ignorance that I protest with all my might!" said Adele with vehemence. "It is that that is unfair. It makes me ridiculous."

"I don't see the sense of it myself," agreed Vestalia, simply. "I always thought it would be the simplest course to tell you everything at once. Or no— what have I said?" she hastened to add, in deprecation of the other's kindling eye; "I didn't feel that way at first. It was I who originally suggested that you shouldn't be told, at the start. I was afraid of you, you know. But now I feel quite differently. I would gladly have you know everything— but your father has other views. It is his secret, now, much more than it is mine. I don't think there is any reason why I shouldn't tell you that much."

"Oh-h!" groaned Adele, in wrath at her helplessness. "Well, tell me this, anyway, how long is this tomfoolery to be kept up?"

"No, don't ask me," answered Vestalia, sympathetically at last. "I don't know. I can only say that I'm as tired of it now as you are. I wish you would believe that. It would make me easier in my mind."

"Well, I do believe it, then," the dark girl replied, with impulsive readiness. "Oh, and something occurs to me that I daresay you can tell me. You remember the day at the Museum. Well, the gentleman who was with you called here next day, papa having in the meantime seen you secretly, downstairs. Now, papa seemed clearly annoyed with that gentleman, when he came up and found him here. Now, why was that?"

Vestalia reflected. It was evident enough that the question honestly puzzled her. "All I can think of," she replied, after consideration, "is that your father had taken it for granted that this gentleman was my husband— and when it came out in our interview that he wasn't then your father questioned me very closely about him, and it happened that it was a subject upon which I couldn't very well tell him much, and I daresay he formed an unfavorable opinion of Mr. Mosscrop on that account. That is the only explanation I can think of. I know he said he thought it would be well for me not to see him again, or even hold communication with him— but I did write him a letter that very day all the same."

It was Adele's turn to ponder. "But why," she began, hesitatingly, "why should papa take it upon himself to tell you what to do and not to do? What business is it of his? And, if he disliked the thing, why should he remain friendly to you, and snub the gentleman you call Mr. Mosscrop? Not that he minded it, or that it amounted to anything, but it puzzles me that papa should behave in that curious fashion."

"Yes, it would have been more natural to show the woman the cold shoulder, and think nothing amiss of the man," assented Vestalia, gravely. "I quite agree with you there."

"Well, that is the way of the world, isn't it?" put in Adele, in apologetic tones. "Don't dream that I suggest anything wrong."

"Oh no," said the other patiently, but with a note of weariness in her voice. "It doesn't matter, one way or the other."

"You love him, then?" Adele's black eyes glowed with a sudden kindly warmth which went to Vestalia's heart.

"Oh, how can I tell you?" she faltered. "It is all so stupid— and I am so unhappy? He was goodness itself to me, and he must think that I behaved like a brute— a common girl of the streets— or meaner still, for at least it's said they have some sense of gratitude. He came like Providence itself to help me, when I was absolutely starving and turned out of doors like a dog— and I was grateful, and yet here he must be thinking that I'm the very scum of the earth!"

She gazed at her companion out of swimming eyes, and for answer Adele kissed her.

"I will go now," she stammered, hastily, as if the caress had further unnerved her. "I've stayed longer than I meant. Yes, I will come again— if you tell your father that I've been, and he says I may come."

"I'd like to see him say anything else!" cried the young lady from Paris, Kentucky. "The idea!"

And when the door had closed upon Vestalia, this dark beauty clenched her hands, and strode indignantly about the room, and repeated between set teeth, "The very idea!"

Chapter 11

Vestalia paused at the street entrance of the hotel, and looked doubtfully up the hill toward the shifting outline of the strident, crowded Strand.

The prospect repelled her, and she bent her slow steps in the other direction. Crossing the empty, sun-baked roadway of the Embankment, she strolled westward in the partial shade of the young lime-trees, which maintain a temerarious existence along the line of the river's parapet.

She looked over the stonework to the water from time to time as she walked, and every glance instinctively wandered up-stream toward the stretch of Westminster Bridge, poised delicately in the noonday haze across the body of the sleepy flood. The stately beauty of the opposing piles of buildings which it linked one with the other, and brought together into the loftiest picture the Old World knows, came as she moved toward it to soothe and uplift her spirits. Her lips parted with pleasure at the spectacle, and at the thought that there, in that glorious span between St. Thomas' and St. Stephen's, her own romance had been born.

The warm serenity of the scene, the inimitable composure of its vast parts, lying under the sunshine in such majestic calm, seemed to chide the weak flutterings and despondencies to which she had surrendered her bosom. The romance which absorbed her mind, of which, indeed, her whole being had become a portion, had its home there, in the heart of that benignant grandeur. The grace and charm and noble strength of what she gazed upon rebuked her timid want of confidence in Destiny, as it shapes itself on Westminster Bridge. She walked forward with a firmer step, her head up, and her eyes drying themselves by the radiance of their own glance.

And so, being borne along by the powerful spell which this great vista has cast about her, she had no sense of surprise when it caught up also David Mosscrop in its train, and placed him at her side. It was at the corner of the bridge, and a momentary clustering of pedestrians brought to a stand-still by a policeman's uplifted hand had diverted her thoughts, and then someone touched her on the arm.

She turned and drank in what had happened with tranquil, tenderly self-possessed eyes. She gave no start, as of a mind caught unawares. She was conscious of no wonder, no tremor of disturbance at the unexpected. The luminous regard in which she embraced the newcomer was as unreasoningly ready for him as are the spontaneous raptures of dreamland. No words came to her lips, but it was in the air that she had known he was coming.

"I was just going to hunt a fellow up at his club across there," said Mosscrop, his coarser masculine sense suggesting an explanation, "and I chanced to look over here, and I made sure it was you, and——"

He stopped short too, and the slower fires kindled in the glance which met hers. They looked into each other's eyes, in a long moment of silence. He drew her arm in his, while the glamour of this sustained gaze rested still upon them. Then, with a lengthened happy sigh she spoke.

"I want to go again to that dear little place where we breakfasted," she said softly. "You must let me have my own way. I have money in my purse, now, and you must come and lunch with me. And it must be— oh, it must be there."

They drove there, this time in a high-hung, sumptuous, noiseless hansom, which sped with an entranced absence of motion through the busy streets.

"It is like fairyland again," she whispered, nestling against him in the narrow, deeply-padded enclosure. And he, resting his hand upon hers under the shelter of the closed doors, breathed heavily, and murmured a cadence without words in ecstatic response.

In some ridiculous fraction of time they were at their journey's end. The impression of having traveled on a magic carpet was in their minds as, almost ruefully, they woke from their daydream of arrow-flight through space, stepped out, and paid the cabman. They laughed together at the thought, without necessity of mentioning what amused them.

Vestalia, before they entered the restaurant, drew her companion a few doors up the street, and halted before the narrow window of the old French bootmaker's shop. Here they laughed again, he merrily, she with a lingering, mellow aftermath of feeling in her tone.

It was only when they were seated in the little room above and she had drawn off her gloves, and after a joyous insistence upon doing it all herself, had chosen some dishes from the card and sent the waiter off with the order, that their tongues were loosened.

David leaned back in his chair, and beamed broad content. He began to talk in the measured, smooth-flowing tone which she remembered so well. "First of all, dear girl," he said, "I want to put on the record my boundless delight at finding you once more. I take off my hat to the gods. They have devised in my behalf a boon which swallows up all the imaginable ills of a lifetime. I swear to complain of nothing they do for the rest of my days. They have given you back to me; and if I am dull enough to lose you again, why, I will bow my head submissively to the deserved mishaps of an ass."

The girl's blue eyes twinkled with a soft, glad light. "It is a great joy to hear your voice again," she said, gently. "The echoes of it have kept up a little faint murmur in my ears ever since we parted, as if some spirit was holding a phantom shell close to my head. And now it is as if we hadn't parted at all, isn't it?— I mean, for the present."

"Ah, it matters so little what you mean," he replied, in affectionate banter. "I erred once, to my profound misfortune, in deferring to your mental processes, and permitting them to translate themselves into actions. Do not think that I shall be so weak again. The key shall never fail to be turned on you hereafter."

She laughed gaily, and shook her head in playful defiance. "Ah, but suppose——" she began, and then let a glance of merry archness complete her sentence.

"I confess to curiosity," he said. "I should prize highly your conception of the motives which prompted you to run away from me."

Her mood sobered perceptibly. "I did it because it was right."

"As a mainspring of human action, that is inadequate," he commented. "Almost all painful and embarrassing things are right, but wise people avoid them as much as possible none the less."

"No, it was right for me to go," she persisted. "I couldn't stay and be dependent upon someone else, no matter who that someone else was. Your kindness to me that whole day was more grateful to me than you can think. I was so frightened in that early morning there on the bridge, so desolate and helpless and sick with dread of what was going to become of me, that I didn't dream of hesitating to take shelter in your— your friendship. It was like going under some hospitable roof while there was a drenching rain outside, and I was very thankful for the refuge. But when it cleared up, I couldn't go on staying, just because I had been made welcome, now, could I?"

"Since you ask me, I declare with tearful emphasis that you could."

"No, seriously," urged Vestalia; "don't you agree with me that women should be just as self-reliant and independent as men?"

"Me? I agree absolutely. I would have women insist upon the most unflinching independence, all the world over. I feel so keenly on that point, that out of the entire sex I would make only one exception. Very few people would take such an advanced position as that, I imagine. Just fancy how far I go! There are hundreds of millions of women, and I would have them all independent but just one. By a curious accident it happens that you are that one— but you will be fair-minded enough to recognize, I feel convinced, that this is the merest chance."

She made a droll little mouth at him, and he went on:

"Yes, it is very strange. I cannot pretend to account for it, but you do undoubtedly form an exception to what would otherwise be a universal rule. The thought of other women earning their own living fills me with joy. I am fascinated by it, I assure you. I feel like bursting into song at the barest suggestion of the idea. But this very excess of reverence for the general principle begets a corresponding vehemence of feeling about the one solitary exception. That is in accordance with a natural law. Surely you respect natural laws? Well, the vaguest adumbration of an idea of your doing things for yourself convulses me with rage. The notion that my right to take entire charge of you is disputed seems monstrous and abominable to me. It is a denial of my mission on earth, and I am bound to combat it with all my powers."

Vestalia smiled. "I see what you mean. You are just an old prehistoric savage like the rest of your sex. Your one idea is to drag a woman off into your cave and keep her there, with a big rock rolled up in front of the door when you're away."

"I would not have you disparage the primitive instincts," urged Mosscrop, with an air of solemnity. "My word for it, we should be an extraordinarily uninteresting lot without them. They are the abiding bone and flesh and muscle of humanity, upon which it pleases each foolish generation in turn to stretch its own thin, trivial pelt of fashionable convention. My desire to seize you, and drag you off to my own cave, and make a life's business of keeping you there, always beautiful, always happy, always replenishing the wellspring of joy in my existence— you choose that as something typical of the primeval man surviving within me. Let me tell you, sweet little Vestalia, that the human mind would cease tomorrow from its eternal wistful dream of progress if it were not for the hope that advancing civilization will bring improved facilities for that sort of thing. The world would wilt, and curl up like a sapless leaf, and drop from its solar stem into gaseous space, if that anticipation were taken away. The race keeps itself going only by cherishing the faith that sometime, somewhere in the golden future, this planet will be arranged so that the right woman will always get into the right cave. That is what people mean when they speak of the millennium."

"That is all very well," said Vestalia, "but it deals with everything from the man's point of view. Consider the other side of the case. What do you say to the woman's disinclination for cave-life— is that not entitled to respect?"

"Possibly," answered David, reflectively— "if one were able to believe in it."

The waiter entered at this point with a burdened tray in his arms, and Vestalia took up the wine list. "Which is it that we had — that in the lovely high green bottles, with arms like a vase?" she asked Mosscrop. "We must have the same again."

"You have told me nothing as yet," said David, reproachfully, when they were alone again, "of all the thousand things I long to know."

"It is so hard to tell," she explained, with hesitation. "That is, there are things that I am supposed not to tell to anybody, at present, at least. And as for what I ought not to tell you— why I have been instructed to avoid you altogether. I was even told not to write you— but I did all the same— just once."

David took a crumpled envelope from an inner pocket over his heart, held it up for her inspection, and replaced it. But even as he did so somber shadows began to gather on his face. He laid down his knife and fork, and, biting his lips, looked out of the window.

Vestalia swiftly recalled gruesome associations with that look. She stretched forth her hand, and laid it on his arm. "You mustn't look out there," she protested. "It has a bad effect on you. Look me in the face instead— please!"

He shook his head impatiently, and stared with dogged, blinking eyes at the opposite roofs. "You don't realize what it has all meant to me," he said at last, his gaze still averted. The quaver in his voice profoundly affected the girl.

"Listen to me—David," she said, with something of his pathos reflected in her tone. "Turn and look at me. I haven't the heart for even a moment of misunderstanding today. There isn't anything on earth I won't tell you. But you must look at me!"

He slowly obeyed her, and she saw that there were tears in his eyes. "But apparently there are things which it would be merciful not to tell me," he said, struggling for an instant for composure. Then his brows knitted themselves, and flashes played in the darkness of his glance.

"Who forbids you this or that?" he demanded, the angry metallic growl rising in his voice. "Four days ago you were all alone in the world! You told me so! In detail you assured me of your isolation. What are you talking about now? You speak of receiving instructions— to avoid me altogether, to write no letter to me! Oh, I ask for no explanations——" he went on stormily, pushing back his chair to rise from the table— "don't think I claim any right to question you. But I find myself mistaken, that is all! I am a silly duffer at a game of this sort. I take things in earnest, while the others are laughing in their sleeves. Well, I've had my lesson. Before God, I'll never——"

Vestalia screamed at him. She had half-risen in her place, gazing with bewildered, frightened eyes, till some vague inkling of his meaning dawned upon her brain. "Foolish David! Foolish!" she cried aloud now. "Stop it! Stop it! You don't know what you're saying! Keep still, and let me talk to you!"

She bent across the table, and peremptorily shook his shoulder to enforce her words. "You're all wrong!" she clamored, as his tempest of wrathful words subsided. Upon the silence which followed she implanted firmly the added comment: "Oh, you goose!"

He looked up sullenly to her, as she stood now erect— and, meeting the glance in her eyes, felt himself clinging to it. There was for him the effect of sunshine in it— of clouds parted, of radiance and calm restored about him. Breathing hard, he gazed into her face, and came somehow to know from what he saw in it that he had been making a fool of himself. This perception assumed sharp outlines in his mind before she had spoken a word.

"Now, will you behave yourself, and listen to me?" she demanded, with austerity. His shattered aspect of contrition was a sufficient answer, and she seated herself confidently.

"Now I will explain things to you— although you don't deserve it in the very least," she began, in formal tones. "To commence with, you remember that American father and daughter that we met at the Museum, down in the basement?— well, it happened that— happened that— Oh, my poor boy, how could you think so stupidly of me?"

David had drawn up to his place again. He held Vestalia's hands in his at this juncture, somehow, and the enchanted table narrowed itself until there was no barrier of space between their lips.

The little kiss sweetened the air. The two, even while they exchanged a glance of shy surprise, thought of it with reverence. They instinctively gave to its contemplation a moment of tender silence.

"How shrewd you were in discerning my leaven of savagery," he remarked at last. "Or leaven? we'd better say principal ingredient!"

"I like you that way," said Vestalia, quietly.

He smiled at her in dreamy incredulity. "I wonder if you do," he mused. "They say women do like men who beat them. The police courts seem to support the idea. But there is a difficulty, you see. If you liked me because I behaved badly to you, then I should dislike you on precisely that account. So you mustn't suggest approbation. No, I was very rude and stupid, and I am profoundly ashamed of myself. I should be ashamed to offer an excuse, too, if it were not just the one it is. I happen to be head over heels in love with you, dear little lady."

"And precisely what is that an excuse for?" demanded the girl, with a fine show of ingenuous calm.

"For letting my luncheon get cold," he replied, taking up his fork.

With the laughter of pleased children, they resumed the broken course of the meal.

"It doesn't begin to be as nice as your breakfast," she commented after a little.

"I don't think it is a day for things to eat," he said, pushing the plate aside. "I want to do nothing but just look at you— perhaps talk a little— but hear you talk much more. I am conscious of an indefinite hunger for the mere visual charm of you, sitting there opposite me. It seems as if it would take years to satisfy that alone. Do you know that you are very beautiful, dear, in your new clothes?"

She regarded his face with a keen, almost anxious glance, before she let the softer look dominate her own. "I am going to hurry to tell you where I got them," she said. "They are the gift of my uncle— my father's brother. This was what I was beginning to explain when— when you got so unhappy."

"Yes— that is the merciful word— unhappy," he assented,

with gratitude. "I have been deeply out of sorts— mentally— since I lost you that night. There is a special devil inside of me, Vestalia, who sometimes lies low for long periods, and hardly reminds me of his existence, but since last Thursday he has been out on the war-path, night and day. My nerves are stretched like fiddle-strings, just with the effort of holding him. The sight of you is death to him, dear. He is gone now— clean out of existence. And while you stay, he won't return. But the wretch has left me tired and a little tremulous. I want to rest myself by just looking at you."

She, smiling with demure pleasure at his speech and his look, related to him briefly the story of the Skinner pedigree. "It occurred to me the minute I woke up in the early morning," she declared. "I shall always believe that I really dreamed it first. Are you interested in dreams?"

"Oh immensely— at the time."

"No; but there is something in them. I assure you, the idea never entered my head the day we met them. But before I was fairly awake next morning, lo, there it was, all worked out. The old gentleman was politeness itself. He came down immediately, when I sent my note upstairs. When I told him about wanting to make a pedigree of the Skinners, the notion appealed to him at once. Then I told him about something else, and that appealed to him a good deal more."

Vestalia paused here, and began to regard her companion with signs of diminishing confidence. "I can't go any farther without making a most humiliating confession to you," she faltered.

"Then don't go any farther, I beseech you," he answered. "Truly, I do not find myself stirred very much by this entire demonstration of your ability to do things off your own bat. It is independent and praiseworthy and all that, no doubt, but I still have a lingering feeling that you ought to have stayed to breakfast, you know, and left mere commercial details to me. And I certainly shrink from humiliating confessions. Skip the unpleasant parts. We will have no skeletons at our feast today."

"Ah, but they can't be skipped," sighed Vestalia. She drew nearer to him, across the table, and lowered her voice. "I foolishly told you some things that were not so— that first morning," she confided in doleful tones. "It was a kind of romance about myself that I had built up in my own mind, and without much thought I gave it to you as truth. So long as I kept it to myself it did no harm; it even made life easier and more endurable for me, like a poor child making-believe that she and her rag doll are princesses. But it was different to tell you. My father was not a French gentleman. He was not an officer, and he wasn't killed in a duel. He was never in France any more than I was. My mother was Scotch, but she did not belong to any noble or wealthy family. She did not leave any family jewels with a crest on them, and no one cheated her out of a private fortune, because she never had such a thing. It was just my individual fairyland that I described to you as real. I didn't even tell you my true name."

David smiled solace upon her distressed aspect "You speak as if it were of importance. Dear child, do we value a rare and beautiful lily the less, because the gardener has put the wrong label on it by mistake? Tut—tut! Names and lineage and all that— it is the idlest stuff on earth to me. The story that you told me was pleasant in my ears only because it came from your lips. The discovery now that it was all yours— that it was not the mere recital of dull facts, but was the child of your own inner imaginings— why that only makes it the more delightful to me. I simply gave it store-room in my memory before; I love it now— and at the same time I find I have quite forgotten it. There is a paradox for you!"

Vestalia essayed a smile through her tears. "You are always kinder than even I expect you to be," she faltered; "but I did tell you a— a story, and by rights you should be very angry with me."

David laughed. "Hans Christian Andersen told me many stories, but I worshiped him increasingly to the end. Dear lady, the stories are the only veritable things in life. The alleged realities of existence pass by us, or roll over us, and leave us colorless and empty. The genuine possessions of our souls— the things that shape and decorate and furnish our spiritual habitations— are the things that never happened. I note a twinkle in your eye. You fancy that I have said an inept thing. You think that I shall have to go back and explain that at least what has happened to us forms an exception to the rule. Ah, sweet little Vestalia, have you forgotten your own remark, here in this very room? 'It isn't like real life at all,' you said; 'it is the way things happen in fairy tales.' I take my stand upon that definition. We have deliberately repudiated what are described as the realities of life. We discard them, cut them dead, decline to have anything whatever to do with them. We declare that it is fairyland that we are living in, and that we refuse to come out of it to the end of our days."

Vestalia gazed into his eyes with wistful tenderness. "To the end of our days!" she murmured softly, wonderingly. Then she recalled the task still unfinished. "I took the name of Peaussier," she forced herself to continue, "because it was a translation of my own name. I looked in the dictionary, and found that it was the French for Skinner."

David lifted his brows. "You don't mean——" he began, confusedly.

"Yes;" she forestalled his question. "The old gentleman at the Savoy is my father's own brother. My father was Abram Skinner. He was not a lucky man, or, in his later years, a very nice man either. He was always poor, and toward the end he was in other troubles too. My home was a thing to shudder at the recollection of. I ran away from it after mother died, and he's gone, too, now. I changed the name, to wash my hands of the whole miserable thing. And then to think of the wonderful chance— to stumble upon my own uncle, a man of fortune and education, and the kindest heart alive— is it not the most extraordinary thing that ever happened in this world?"

"Very possibly it might be regarded as extraordinary— out in the so-called world," David assented, reflectively. "But it is just the thing that would be expected in fairyland. Yes, it seems, on the face of it, a beneficent occurrence. It is good for you to be seized and possessed of a rich uncle— from some points of view. But from others— a doubt suggests itself, Vestalia, whether your uncle is well-affected toward the fairies. Standard Oil does not lend itself without an effort to the fantastic. What if your uncle beckons you to come forth from fairyland?"

"And leave you behind— is that what you mean?" asked Vestalia, slowly. "That would depend— depend on how much you wanted me to stay."

David put out his left hand to take hers, where it lay upon the cloth. With his right he drew out his watch. "The name Skinner," he said, "is all right for the folk at the Savoy. It is not a suitable name for you. I sympathize fully with your impulse to abandon it. The expedient which you adopted was, no doubt, the best that offered itself at the moment, but I think I know a better. I must leave you now, and hurry into the City. This is Monday. Dear love, on Thursday I claim the whole day from you. We will breakfast here at eight— it is not too early, is it?— or say rather that at just eight I will come and find you on Westminster Bridge. The day must begin there, mustn't it? And— strangely enough— Thursday is in a sort another birthday of mine."

"And of mine too?" she asked, with a light in her eyes.

Chapter 12

In the early afternoon of Thursday, David Mosscrop walked apart on shaded gravel-paths, beneath arches of roses and the feathered canopy of cedars high above, with Adele by his side.

"Oh, it's all right. The waiter will come out and tell us when it is ready," he said reassuringly, in comment upon her backward glance. "I want to speak with you. There was no such thing as a word with you by yourself on the road."

"Why, we talked every mortal minute," she protested.

"Ah yes, we talked, but I don't recall that anything was said."

"I daresay my conversation is empty to the last degree," she observed; "but I am usually spared such frank statements of the fact."

"Ah, but I want to be thought of as something a little different from the usual," urged David.

"Your efforts in that direction have been extraordinarily successful. Pray, do not imagine that they are unappreciated. I admit freely that you seem to have quite exhausted the unusual, my Lord."

"No; I've still got something up my sleeve," said David, lightly enough. But the tone in which she had uttered those final two words caught his attention. They carried a suggestion of emphasis which fell outside the bounds of genial banter. Meditating upon it he stole a covert glance at her, and encountered two wide-awake black eyes intently scrutinizing him in turn. "It was about that I wished to consult you," he added, conscious of an embarrassed tongue.

"Won't it be better to stick to scenery?" she asked. Yes, there was undoubtedly a mocking touch in her voice. "That is so safe a subject. This dear old hotel here, now, how perfectly satisfying it is! Those wonderful trees out in front, and the white chalk hill behind, and this garden, and then the comfort and charm of everything inside, and the thought that people have been coming here for hundreds of years, or is it thousands?— it is so different from anything we have in America— even in Kentucky. And then the whole drive from London— through such delicious country, all so rich and smooth and neatly packed together, and so full of the notion that people are all the while planting and pruning and admiring every inch of it that you can't help feeling affectionately toward it yourself! Perhaps there is a certain hint of the artificial about it, but somehow that seems rather in keeping with the day than otherwise, doesn't it, my Lord?"

While he hesitated about an answer, she touched him on the arm. "Here are papa and Mr. Linkhaw coming along after us— probably to tell us luncheon is ready. Shan't we wait for them?"

"Heavens, no!" cried David, starting forward. "We've been chained to them on the top of the coach for two whole hours," he went on, in defensive explanation of his warmth. "Really, we have earned the right to a few quiet words by ourselves."

"Oh, I don't mind," said Adele, quickening her pace to suit his. "Only it's fair to warn you, though, that my temper has its limitations. I am a variable person. Sometimes it happens that all at once I weary of a joke, after it has been carried to a certain length, and then I can be as unpleasant as they make them."

"I find that my own sense of humor has a tendency to flag under sustained effort, as I get older," said David. "But there are so many pleasantries afloat— perhaps you wouldn't mind indicating the one which particularly fatigues you, and I will put my foot on it at once."

"Oh, by no means! That would be far too crude. We are all your guests, and you are in charge of the entertainment, and I couldn't dream of suggesting anything."

"Except that you find yourself no longer amused," ventured David, cautiously.

"Oh. not at all." She spoke with perfunctory languor, and simulated a little yawn. "I daresay it is all immensely funny, only I got up earlier than usual this morning, and no doubt that has dulled my wits somewhat."

David perceived on the instant how matters stood. "I also rose at an extravagantly early hour and it is about my reasons for doing so that I want to tell you. But, first of all, let us be frank with each other. I have done nothing but accede to a situation created for me by Archie and yourself. It has been within your power to end it at any moment you choose. It has been all along much more your joke than mine. It isn't fair to round on me for merely humoring your own conception of sport."

Adele halted momentarily, and surveyed his composed, swarthy countenance with lifted brows. "So you saw all along that I knew!" she exclaimed, in honest surprise.

"How could I have imagined that so clumsy a performance as

mine would deceive so clever a young woman?" he rejoined, with a sprightly bow.

"Oh, you did it awfully well," she assured him, complacently. "But tell me, did Archie suspect that I knew?"

"I have been intimate with Archie from the cradle," said David, "but I am still very shy about forming opinions as to his mental processes. In this case, however, I think it is safe to say he didn't suspect— and still doesn't suspect."

"Poor old Archie," mused Adele, with a ripening smile. "I knew who he was before I'd even laid eyes on him. A school-friend of mine in Galveston wrote to me that she had met a real Earl, who insisted on being known as Mr. Linkhaw, and that he was returning to England by way of Kentucky. I've had three months of the rarest fun in never letting on that I had the remotest suspicion. You can't imagine how comical it was. He used to get, quite tearful sometimes, I abused the aristocracy so fiercely. And then, the joke was, papa began— his whole idea of conversation is to take up today what I've said yesterday, and multiply my words by a hundred and twelve, and produce the result as his own; and he worked up the anti-Earl agitation till Archie very nearly went off into chronic melancholia. It was better than any comedy that ever was written— but then you stumbled your way into the middle of it, and got it all twisted and tangled up— and it hasn't been so amusing since then."

"My dear Miss Skinner," protested David, "I think my entrance upon the scene deserves a gentler verb. If you will search your memory, you will find that I came in by express invitation. It was you who deliberately thrust my mock honors upon me."

"Oh, I know that," she responded, readily enough. "I thought that would only make the thing funnier still— but somehow it hasn't. It isn't anything about Archie and me, you know. But there is another element in the case that I feel very keenly about. It has been puzzling me for days, but I only learned the truth last night. I simply made papa tell me. I refused flat-footed to come here today, or to do anything else that was reasonable, unless he did tell me. I have a cousin here in England, Mr. Mosscrop, a daughter of my father's own brother, and she is one of the dearest girls that ever lived."

"I can readily credit that," declared David, pointing his meaning with a little inclination of the head.

"Oh, she is far nicer than I am," cried Adele. "She wouldn't trifle with the feelings of the man she loved, or play tricks with him just for the sake of fun. In fact, I almost blame her for taking such things too seriously. She hasn't had too easy a time of it, poor girl, and it has made her, I think, altogether too humble. She met a young man in the midst of her troubles who, it seems, was civil to her, and even kind as men go, and what does she do but just sit down and worship the very memory of him, and cry out her pretty blue eyes over it— and he— he walks off and never gives her another thought. That's the man of it!"

A gleam of indignation flashed through the moisture in her own eyes as she bent them upon her companion. Her bosom heaved the more as she discerned a broad smile extending itself upon his face.

"Although I might demur to details," he said, restraining the gaiety which struggled for expression in his voice, "I must not pretend to fail to recognize the portrait you have drawn. I am the guilty man!"

"You laugh at it!" she exclaimed. "To you it seems a joke!"

"Are you so certain that there isn't a joke concealed somewhere about it?" he suggested, calmly.

"I lose patience with you! You make a jest of everything. Tell me this much: Do you or do you not know her present address?"

"I know precisely where she is to be found at the present moment," said David, speaking now with gravity.

"Well, and have you been there to see her? Have you written to her there? Have you given her the slightest sign since she has been there of any desire on your part to ever see her again?"

"I must answer 'No' to each question, I am afraid," he responded, and had the grace to hang his head.

His evident humility only momentarily impressed her. "I am disappointed in you," she said. "Where will you find a sweeter or truer woman? Don't think I am throwing her at your head! Quite the contrary. If you were to ask for her now, I should advise with all my might against you. But you have behaved like a simpleton. I am going to have her always live with me, or near me. She is my own flesh and blood, and I love her as if she were my sister. She doesn't know, as yet, that I am aware of the relationship; but I have written to her this very morning, telling her to come and see me tonight, when I get back. I am going to spend some money in Scotland."

"It will be profoundly appreciated, believe me."

She sniffed at his interjection. "I intend to buy land right and left in Elgin, and if Skirl Castle isn't good enough— I don't think much of it from the photographs—we'll build a bigger one, and we'll make that whole section hum; and Vestalia shall be as big an heiress as it contains, and the lucky man who marries her shall be treated like a brother of mine and Archie's. And that is what you have thrown away. I say it to you frankly, because it is all over so far as you are concerned. She will listen to me, and my mind is quite made up— and papa can tell you what that means!"

"Even if your decision were not irrevocable," said David, solemnly, "my answer would of necessity be the same. I would do much to please you, but I do not see my way to marrying your cousin."

They had paused to exchange these last sentences, and now upon the instant the Earl and his elderly companion came up. David essayed a revelatory wink to the nobleman, but it fell upon the stony places in Lord Drumpipes wondering stare.

Mr. Skinner wiped his brow decorously, and breathed appreciation of the halt. "Sir," he began, addressing David, "I must assume that I am enjoying the opportunity of studying a district of England peculiarly favored by Nature, and exceptionally embellished as well by the hand of man; but I wish to give expression to emotions of unmixed delight at all that I observe about me. We have inspected the internal appointments of the ancient hostelry, and have reveled, sir, in the luxurious yet studiously regulated beauties of this garden, and I confess that the novelty of the one and the charm of the other far surpass anything——"

"Papa," interposed his daughter, with cold severity, "we will leave these gentlemen to enjoy the novelties and charms by themselves for a few minutes, if you please. I have an explanation to make to you, since no one else offers it, and I think it should be no longer deferred."

She took her father's arm as she spoke, and led him in a direct line across the sward toward the broad, low-lying, ivy-clad rear of the hotel. "Oh, it's all right; they don't mind your walking on the grass in England," the two young men heard her say as she departed.

These partners in deception gazed after her for a space. Then they looked at each other.

"Davie, I don't like it," said the Earl.

"Don't like what?"

"I'm afraid she's got some kind of an inkling. It looks as if a suspicion were dawning in her mind. I warned you she was keen of scent."

Mosscrop burst forth with a peremptory guffaw of laughter. "You duffer of the earth," he cried, "she knew all about you before ever she laid eyes on you!" He unfolded the chuckling narrative forthwith, to the Earl's profound astonishment and concern.

"Why then, man," Drumpipes ejaculated at last, staring hard at the close-cropped lawn, "I can't tell in the least if she loves me for myself alone."

"Oh, you read that in some novel," objected David. "It's a mere phrase; it has no significance in real life."

"Yes; but," the other pursued, dejectedly, "I don't see how I can make sure that she loves me in any kind of way."

"At all events, she's going to marry you," David re-assured him. "She mentioned the fact to me, casually. And she's going to buy up Elgin right and left, and build a new Skirl Castle as big as Olympia, and generally make everything else north of the Grampians 'sing small'— I believe that's the phrase."

The Earl assimilated this intelligence with a kindling eye. "Man, it's fine!" he cried, as the prospect spread itself out before his mental vision. "Ah, poor Davie, you dinna ken what it is to be in love!"

Mosscrop sighed. "When you talk Scots, Archie," he said, "I know it's going to cost me money. I foresee that you'll kick about the bill. But, hurry, man, and catch up with them. She's quite capable of flouncing out of the house, and dragging her father along, too, while the fit is on her; and that would only mean more bother to coax them back. Come on!"

He started at a brisk pace in pursuit, and Drumpipes strode eagerly beside him. They overtook their guests on the very threshold of the door, and the Earl called out a breathless, entreating "Adele!" The girl, upon reflection, turned, and surveyed the pair with an austere eye.

"Wait a moment, papa," she said in her coldest tone; "one of these two gentlemen seems to feel authorized to address me by my Christian name, and apparently has also some communication to make to us."

"Well," stammered Drumpipes, hesitatingly, "there's an awfully good luncheon been ordered, you know."

Mosscrop emitted an abrupt, resonant note of laughter, and in the silence which ensued displayed violent muscular efforts to keep a grin from convulsing his face.

Adele preserved the severity of her aspect for a little. "I think it might occur to you, Lord Drumpipes," she began, markedly addressing her remarks to the rightful bearer of the title, "that after what has happened— and on this point, I can assure you my father feels exactly as I do——"

She stopped here, with the effect of appealing to her father for immediate confirmation of their inflexible joint attitude.

"I need scarcely observe," began Mr. Skinner, putting up his pince-nez and looking down upon the two young men with sternness from the vantage of the door-step, "that whatever course my daughter deems it consistent with her dignity to pursue, in the face of the extraordinary, and, I may confidently add, unprecedented circumstances which we are called upon to—to confront, has my most unswerving adhesion."

A waiter opened the door inward at this instant, and overlaid Mr. Skinner's peroration with a clear-cut message, Germanic in its non-essentials, but broadly human in import.

The old gentleman gasped, twiddled the string of his glasses in his fingers, and leaned his head sidewise toward his daughter. "Yes, but what is it we're going to do?" he inquired in a nervous whisper.

"Do?" cried Mosscrop, who had caught her glance in his own, and convicted it of latent merriment, "Do? Why we're going to laugh at a harmless pleasantry happily ended, and pass in to luncheon."

"Yes, papa," said Adele, upon consideration, and with a dawning smile upon her lips, "I think that is what we're going to do." When they found themselves standing about the table in the private room, overlooking through open French windows the delightful sunlit garden from which they had come, Mosscrop seized the moment of hesitation about seats to hold up his hand. Though he had been bereft of his borrowed dignities, the air of natural command sat easily upon him.

"I have to ask you for a minute or two of delay," he said. "It will explain itself."

He wrote something on a card as he spoke, and gave it to the waiter with a closely-guarded whisper of injunction. As the servant left the room, David turned to the others with a radiant face.

"Mr. Skinner," he began, "and my younger friends, there is a toast which in England is always drunk standing. It occurs to me to propose it to you, on this single occasion, before we have taken our seats at all. As has been remarked with characteristic perspicacity, the circumstances which we find ourselves called upon to confront are extraordinary in character, and altogether unprecedented. Through the courtesy of my friends, I have for a brief period had devolved upon me the responsibility of behaving, at stated intervals, as a member of the Scotch peerage should behave. I view my deportment throughout this ordeal, in retrospect, with a considerable degree of satisfaction. I have spared no pains to realize my conception of the part. The essential thing about a successful peerage, I take it, is that it should be invested, for ordinary eyes, with a glamour of unreality. A Baron should be perceptibly romantic. A Viscount, if he respects his station should quite envelope himself in the mists of the improbable. As for an Earl, he should live frankly in fairyland. My imagination does not run to Marquises and Dukes, but I think I may say I have grasped the ideal of an Earl."

"The true ideal of an Earl," interposed Drumpipes, with inspiration, "is never to let victuals get cold."

Mosscrop smiled and nodded. "Only a minute more," he said. "I spoke about fairyland. I have been under its spell all this week. I have committed myself to its charm for the rest of my days. When you return to London this evening, northward, it is Archie Who will drive you. I go southward to the Loire country instead, under the magic of the enchantment which beckons and guides and propels me, all in one. To quit riddles, good people, you will notice that there is a fifth place laid here before us. To connect this fact with the toast, the seat is waiting for my Queen. This is Sherry, decanted from the 'Anchor's' oldest bin. I suggest to you the filling of your glasses."

He moved toward the door as he spoke, opened it, and turned to the others, with Vestalia on his arm.

"Mr. Skinner," he said gently. "We crave your approbation for what we have done. We were married by the registrar of St. Dunstan's at ten o'clock this morning, and your niece came on here direct by train, bringing her luggage and my own, which I thank God devoutly will always travel together in future. We love each other very, very much."

There fell here upon the masculine vision the spectacle of two women entwined in each other's arms, and of two beautiful heads, one raven-black, one glowing like light through clouded amber, bent tenderly together. The sound of little moans proceeded from this swaying, interlocked group, and then of kisses and of subdued ecstatic sobbing laughter.

Lord Drumpipes, staring vacantly from these women to his boyhood friend, gulped his sherry in an absent-minded way. David, in rapid whispers, outlined meanwhile the situation to his bewildered ear.

"Eh!" he called out at last. "It is the same lassie? The yellow-haired one? The one who smashed my moosie?"

"Shut up, you loon!" growled David fiercely, under his breath. "Is this the time to blab about such things? I kicked your your old cow into splinters, and I'll serve the rest of the idiotic show the same way if you mention the word 'moose.' Chuck it, man! That's a thing for the girls to tell each other a year hence, perhaps. Have some delicacy about you!" He turned to Mr. Skinner, who stood as one petrified, his gaze riveted upon the young women.

"I've been explaining to my friend, Lord Drumpipes," David said, lifting his voice, "the romantic nature of my acquaintance with your niece, my wife. I think you have been told about it."

Mr. Skinner shifted his glance to the speaker. "To some extent — to some extent," he murmured weakly. "It has taken me greatly by surprise. I scarcely know——-"

David had advanced, and was holding out his hand, with a confident, masterful sort of smile.

"I suppose it's all right," the old gentleman said, sending confused, appealing glances toward his inattentive daughter. "Adele seems not to object— I take it for granted that——"

Adele lifted her head, and drew a protecting arm round Vestalia. "Hold up your chin," she whispered, audibly. "They're nothing to be frightened of. You know everybody except your cousin Archie, and he's only to be feared by creatures who can't shoot back."

The bride, nestling against the other's shoulder, raised a luminous face, and looked about her with a smile of frank happiness.

"Frightened?" she queried, and then shook her fair head joyously in answer.

The waiter came in with the tureen.

Harold Frederic

March Hares

Harold Frederic